Dan

About the Author

Treyce d'Gabriel-Montoya is originally from Tucson, Arizona and has over 23 years of experience in Handwriting Analysis. Since 1987 Treyce has been featured on many radio and television talk shows and in written media. She is an internationally recognized as a case consultant and trainer for various agencies including law enforcement, school, behavioral health, human resource, attorney, and more.

During the past 23 years she has been involved in many memorable events. For examples, she helped write the "Higher Power" episode for the popular CBS show <u>Criminal Minds</u>. This episode was about suicide in which she supplied all the samples and helped educate the writers on the appropriate verbiage. Her three most memorable cases include warning a woman that her husband could brutally murder her – a year later, he did. Another when she stated a sheriff deputy was dangerous – he later killed his girlfriend. Another when she stated a Homicide Investigator was dangerous and should not be trusted with children – he was later convicted of six counts of Child Battery. She also has enjoyed assisting in famous cases such as Michael Jackson & Darlie Routier.

Her proudest moment started in January 2006 and is still on-going. Starting in January 2006, she lead the successful Texas Juvenile Probation Commission research project that was aimed at reducing juvenile recidivism rates via the Handwriting Formation Therapy (HFT) program that she created in 1987. The juveniles that were chosen to participate remained 100% anonymous during the entire six month program. All juveniles drastically improved social skills, grades, and gained self-confidence. Most importantly - to-date, none of these juveniles have reoffended. She is the first analyst in history to create and introduce a program like this. For over 20 years many private children, teens and adults around the world have changed their lives permanently with HFT but she urges you to be aware that there are many "copycat" programs out there. In fact, she copyrighted her program in 1987 and the next known works published was in 2000.

After working in the traditional mental health field most of her life as she continued college, she did not notice many long-term benefits and, because of that, she obtained her Forensic Psychology degree from Kaplan University as an Alpha Beta Kappa graduate but later changed her later degrees to Metaphysical Psychology – a more holistic (and successful) approach.

She is the President of the National Association of Handwriting & Document Experts (NAHDE), is a proud member of *Find Me*, the National Scholar's Honor Society, CHAI, APA, and others. She is a certified teacher and sits on the Advisory Board of the international Spark of Light Villages (Pearl Foundation).

Her books include "Written Violence – the Personality Behind the Pen", "Case Files of a Forensic Handwriting Analyst", "Answers", "The Only Handwriting Analysis Book You Will Ever Need", "Dangerous Ink", "Finding Mr. & Mrs. Write", "What's Going on Upstairs", and more.

Services include custody evaluations, employment & tenant screening, jury selection, pre-parole evaluations, detecting lies & drugs, pre-termination violence assessments, compatibility, progression of suicide, sexual abuse, forgeries, anonymous notes, and much more.

QUICK REFERENCE LIST

Texas Juvenile Probation, KnowGangs, Council of Governments, Southern States Correctional Association, Great Lakes International Gang Investigators Coalition, International Association of Law Enforcement Intelligence Analysts (in USA & Mexico), Regional Organized Crime Information Center (ROCIC), West Virginia Department of Corrections, Arizona Public Defenders Association, Texas Gang Investigators Association, Colorado Law Enforcement Officers Association, Green Dental Lab Human Resources, Montgomery County Sheriff's Department, Durango Police

Department, Dalhart Police Department, Trimmier Elementary School, TruVision Management, Texas Parks & Wildlife, Georgia Bureau of Investigation, Village of Glendale Heights Police Department, Refugio County Juvenile Justice Center, Bell County Precinct 1, Lamar County Juvenile Probation, Arkansas Probation & Parole Association, Harlingen Consolidated ISD, Society of Human Resource Management, Hopkins High School, Geico Auto Crime Investigations, 4theKids, Lost Child Network, Missing & Exploited Children, Louisiana State Police, and many more.

For more about Treyce please visit www.SolveMyCase.com. To contact her directly please email Treyce@Treyce.com.

Special Dedication

This book is especially dedicated to the **individuals and agencies that investigate and work toward the prosecution of those that harm others** - *whether human or animal.* I have an enormous amount of respect for you and believe you are driven by a passion to help others and make a difference. I honor you for persevering even on the most difficult of days. The voices of victims are heard through books, friends, relatives, media, and other avenues which serve as reminders that your work is very much appreciated. This book is just one of those avenues for victims to say *"thank you for not giving up on us".*

Dedications

This book is dedicated to <u>my fellow handwriting analysts</u> and my "team" for years of sharing samples, support, advice, and more.

This book is dedicated to <u>my students</u> who continually make me proud.

This book is dedicated to <u>my clients</u> whose support I truly appreciate.

This book is also dedicated to <u>you</u> for seeking knowledge in this fabulous field. May you be driven to share this knowledge and make a difference in, *and possibly save*, the lives of others.

Author's Acknowledgements

This book would not have been possible without the help of several people:

God for His everyday presence, phenomenal guidance, and protection in my life. Additional thanks to Him for giving me the gift of an amazing husband. Mark is truly the most amazing man I've ever known.

My family members and friends who give me the support and the freedom to pursue my goals.

My animal children whose kisses and playfulness help me break through bouts of writers block.

Table of Contents

Introduction

You probably purchased this book because you are fascinated with the forensics field, addicted to handwriting analysis, are curious or somewhere in the middle. Many shows and books have been written that are "forensic" in nature; this definitely falls under that umbrella. In fact, many criminal investigations you see on the news or read about in newspapers hinge on some portion of forensic investigative tools such as handwriting analysis (HWA).

I decided to write this book because one of the things in my life that I have less than ZERO tolerance for is animal abuse. Alongside that is abuse of the elderly, then babies, etc. There is a STRONG CORRELATION of handwriting traits that show ones potential to be abusive. If you have heard me speak or read any of my previous books, you probably recall my purpose statement behind all of my written materials. This purpose statement is…

"Knowledge is worthless unless it is shared"

And I fully believe that with all of my heart and soul.

Therefore, I have designed this book with general terms and have refrained from using too many industry-specific words. So, whether you have absolutely no HWA experience or are an expert, you will be able to use or learn from this book.

If you have read my other books you will notice that I write as society speaks. I do not like to use fancy terms, complicated descriptions, or the like. I want you to understand what I am visually showing and describing. I believe that, when you understand the content clearly, then those you tell will as well. I understand that everyone is at a different comprehension and literacy level so, as I write, I keep that in mind with the end goal of making the content reader-friendly for all.

However if you need any clarification please contact me at Treyce@Treyce.com. If I am unavailable, one of my friendly staff will be happy to assist you.

Enjoy the book !

Disclaimer

The author or her company accepts no responsibility with regard to the content in this book. These are merely her professional opinions based on over 23 years of experience. Because of the length of time she has been working in this field, she cannot recall all the places where handwriting samples and corresponding knowledge was acquired and any omission or error in citing is purely unintentional. The author, and her affiliates, are not responsible for any legal issues, personal issues (whether emotional, physiological or psychological), or any other actions as a direct or indirect use of this book.

Let's begin by looking at the…

CHARACTERISTICS
of various groups
& abusers….

CHARACTERISTICS of Those That Batter

- At least 70% of those who batter were either battered as children or saw violence occur regularly in their homes. They minimize and deny to themselves about the violence; they project blame onto the victim; it is painful if and when they fully realize what they've done.
- Abusers tend to express "hard" emotions, such as guilt, frustration, hurt, anger, etc. Generally expressing either happiness or anger, but nothing in between. Everything is either wonderful, or there is a violent explosion.
- Batterers tend to be excessively dependent on the victim--they perceive their victim as the only person they can relate to, who understands them, etc., regardless of how much they actually share with them. They have an extraordinary fear of losing the relationship and can go to any lengths (even murder) to keep it.
- Batterers have an exaggerated jealousy around "their woman" having any relationships with other people, such as friends, family members, co-workers. They may even constantly monitor his or her activities. The jealousy generally escalates during the relationship without any aggravation.
- Abusers often experience themselves as powerless in the world and over themselves, regardless of actual life accomplishments or status. They personalize often--they see everything (both good and bad) in their lives, as causing the events in their lives, such as "if you didn't irritate me, I wouldn't have to hit you".
- They often are impulsive--move frequently or change jobs, friends, etc. frequently.
- They have a need to control; they define it as being in control of others--but are not in control of themselves. The control issue usually escalates in the relationship, ("Since this is the only person for me, I'd better make sure s/he doesn't get away".)
- They view themselves as emotionally isolated, especially from others of the same gender. They have no true friends.
- Abusers hold traditional, rigid views of the world; such as, men and women have their "places", men are authority figures and have the right to be in control, women belong at home pregnant, etc.
- Abusers have few to no skills in reducing stress levels, other than battering.
- Note: The behavior of abusers is learned - they have a choice. The victim cannot change the abuser and should not minimize the violence and / or the potential for danger.

© Rural Advocacy Program

Characteristics of Sexual Abusers

☐ Refusal to take responsibility for actions and blames others or circumstances for failures
☐ A sense of entitlement
☐ Low self-esteem
☐ Need for power and control
☐ Lack of empathy
☐ Inability to form intimate relationships with adults
☐ History of abuse
☐ Troubled childhood
☐ Deviant sexual behavior and attitudes

© *Protecting Your Children from Sexual Predators*, by Dr. Leigh M. Baker.

Characteristics of Violent Youth

While there is no foolproof system for identifying potentially dangerous students, the following warning signals that could indicate a youth's potential for harming him/herself or others. **Use it as a checklist**.

1.___ History of tantrums and uncontrollable angry outbursts.
2.___ Commonly uses name calling, cursing or abusive language.
3.___ Commonly makes violent threats when angry.
4.___ Previously brought a weapon to school.
5.___ Background of serious disciplinary problems (school / society).
6.___ History of substance / alcohol abuse or dependency.
7.___ Few or no close friends.
8.___ Preoccupied with weapons, explosives or similar devices.
9.___ History of truancy, suspension or expulsion from school.
10.___ Cruelty to animals.
11.___ Little or no supervision / support from parents or caring adults.
12.___ Witnessed or victim of abuse or neglect in the home.
13.___ Bullied and / or bullies or intimidates peers / children / adults.
14.___ Blames others for difficulties / problems he causes.
15.___ Prefers violent TV shows, movies or musical themes.
16.___ Reads materials with violent themes, rituals and abuse.
17.___ Writes about anger, frustration or 'dark side' of life.
18.___ Involved with gangs / antisocial peers otherwise not accepted.
19.___ Often depressed and / or has significant mood swings.
20.___ Has threatened or attempted suicide.

© *Reprinted with permission from the National School Safety Center*

Characteristics of Cult Groups

Concerted efforts at influence and control lie at the core of cultic groups, programs, and relationships. Many members, former members, and supporters of cults are not fully aware of the extent to which members may have been manipulated, exploited, even abused. The following list of social-structural, social-psychological, and interpersonal behavioral patterns commonly found in cultic environments may be helpful in assessing a particular group or relationship.

- The group displays excessively zealous and unquestioning commitment to its leader and (whether he is alive or dead) regards his belief system, ideology, and practices as the Truth, as law.
- Questioning, doubt, and dissent are discouraged or even punished.
- Mind-altering practices (such as meditation, chanting, speaking in tongues, denunciation sessions, and debilitating work routines) are used in excess and serve to suppress doubts about the group and its leader(s).
- The leadership dictates, sometimes in great detail, how members should think, act, and feel (for example, members must get permission to date, change jobs, marry—or leaders prescribe what types of clothes to wear, where to live, whether or not to have children, how to discipline children, and so forth).
- The group is elitist, claiming a special, exalted status for itself, its leader(s) and members (for example, the leader is considered the Messiah, a special being, an avatar—or the group and/or the leader is on a special mission to save humanity).
- The group has a polarized us-versus-them mentality, which may cause conflict with the wider society.
- The leader is not accountable to any authorities (unlike, for example, teachers, military commanders or ministers, priests, monks, and rabbis of mainstream religious denominations).
- The group teaches or implies that its supposedly exalted ends justify whatever means it deems necessary. This may result in members' participating in behaviors or activities they would have considered reprehensible or unethical before joining the group (for example, lying to family or friends, or collecting money for bogus charities).
- The leadership induces feelings of shame and/or guilt in order to influence and/or control members. Often, this is done through peer pressure and subtle forms of persuasion.

11

- Subservience to the leader or group requires members to cut ties with family and friends, and radically alter the personal goals and activities they had before joining the group.
- The group is preoccupied with bringing in new members.
- The group is preoccupied with making money.
- Members are expected to devote inordinate amounts of time to the group and group-related activities.
- Members are encouraged or required to live and/or socialize only with other group members.
- The most loyal members (the "true believers") feel there can be no life outside the context of the group. They believe there is no other way to be, and often fear reprisals to themselves or others if they leave (or even consider leaving) the group.

© *Janja Lalich, Ph.D. & Michael D. Langone, Ph.D.*

Characteristics of Workplace Violence

Targets of workplace violence can include the self, co-workers, and property. Violence-Suicide is particularly prevalent in certain occupations (e.g., medical, law enforcement) in which high stress is associated with accessibility to the means for achieving death. Violence can be initiated by an employee who reacts to an immediate situation or to a consistent pattern of harassment. Intruder-initiated violence occurs when a non-employee initiates violence in a workplace and typically involves a problematic relationship between the intruder and an employee. This includes domestic violence incidents when pursuing the victim at the worksite.

- A history of violence towards women, children, or animals;
- Self-esteem is highly connected to the job;
- Few interests outside of work;
- Withdrawn and isolated;
- A history of alcohol or drug abuse;
- A history of mental health issues;
- Fascination with violence or weapons.
- Exhibits a sudden change in disposition, quality of work, work habits, or dress
- Shows little tolerance of others
- Intimidates others verbally or physically
- Threatens to harm self or others
- Displays destructive behavior, such as trashing an office, knocking over a desk, or smashing equipment

- Is having domestic problems
- Blames others for failures or disappointments
- Feels frustrated with the job; has low or no job satisfaction
- Recently lost job with no viable options
- Has a history of complaints and grievances
- Has a history of violent or criminal activities
- Talks about violence and killings
- Carries a concealed weapon

© *http://www.mentalhealth.samhsa.gov*

Interview Questions to Elicit Animal Cruelty Histories

1. Are they any pets or other animals in your house?
2. Whose pets / animals are they?
3. What kind? What are their names? How old are they?
4. Who takes care of (animals' name)?
5. Where does (animals name) sleep?
6. What does (animals name) eat?
7. How is (animals' name) disciplined / trained?
8. Does anyone ever hurt (animals' name)? Who? How?
9. Has anyone ever touched (animals' name) sexually? Who? What did (individuals name) do to (animals name)?
10. Have you ever lost a pet that you cared about?
11. Has any animal or pet that you cared about died?
12. Do you worry that something bad will happen to (animals' name)?

© *"Zoo-sadism Questionnaire"*

I'm going to share with you the **most important statements** I was told when I first entered this career as a child over 35 years ago.

I strongly urge you to remember them:

- **Believe** what you see in the handwriting and do <u>not</u> let your subjectivity tell you otherwise. If you see indicators in the handwriting of someone you know – please do <u>not</u> ignore the signs. Sure, he may *"seem like a nice guy"* or she may seem *"incapable of that"* but if it's in the handwriting, it is there for a reason. **That reason may be to save your life!**

- Go with what you see in the handwriting and <u>not</u> with what you want to believe about the individual. Handwriting will <u>not</u> lie to you but **people will.**

- **Listen** to the handwriting and <u>not</u> your heart.

The following section will reveal some of the main "danger indicators" in the handwriting of those that abuse, torture, or kill.

---

tasies...[[no kidding]]... it was the 'older' young women that had far more self-awareness, who literally chi
guys on with no intentions of a real relationship (gold-digger mentality)............That I was interes
hated his 'anyone that'll get in the van' attitude. Such young "girls" (not "women") were/are too naive &
cunt! My preferred age then, was 20-25. Larry and I shouldn't have been involved with one another
crimes! We have/had different interests and motivations. I would've been keen on abducting a really
ly for a month or so (taking great care that she not see me or others) and releasing her. But only those yo
that were haughty (naughty)....oh (?)....bitches! So to speak. And... I knew it was only a fantasy
enjoyable to debate the pros and cons of with other guys who'd had similar fantasies)) Yeah... raw
violism to the max! (but I went to prison for a rape I didn't commit! Yeah!, I'm still &
that — but I didn't go looking for her [a stunning blonde, by-the-way!] when I got out!!) Oh!,,
wisdom of hindsight afterhand !!!

Too perfect (font-like): when the writing is monotonous with no
natural movement instead looking like a computerized font, this
indicates a writer who can easily hide true intentions and, to make up
for the internal feelings of losing control, will control the writing to an
excess. This is the writing of completely unpredictable thoughts and
behaviors making the writer capable of anything – almost always very
violent.

> Very few times in my life can
> I say I was truly happy !
> Maybe I'm not supposed to be !

Excessive lower loops: loops that are too large in comparison to the
rest of the writing size indicate excessive physical energy. The larger in
size the more likely the writer can be physically or sexually aggressive.

> I love myself   I love my mom and
> I love my father and I love my life

Twisted loops: If there are twisted loops in the bottom and / or top of
letters (ie: any lower loop or upper loops or stems of the letters b, d, h,
l, etc.) his sexuality (lower) and / or thoughts (upper) are twisted too!

The writer is then able to justify perverse or aggressive thoughts and behaviors to others who may question it.

I've never had so much to lose than when you threaten to leave my life!

Horizontal loops: when a line seems to cross or lay across the bottom of a lower loop, this indicates a preference for sexual masochism which involves being humiliated, bound, beaten and otherwise made to physically suffer for purposes of sexual stimulation.

I AM SO sorry for hurting you! It WILL NOT HAPPEN AGAIN!

Stencil-like letters: if 80% of more of the letters are disconnected, the more predictably unpredictable the behavior of the writer. What you see is definitely not what you usually get when dealing with this writer. This is the true Dr. Jekyll / Mr. Hyde personality. *If you just see a random letter or two in a sample that indicates anxiety.*

My name is Kristy McKr███ I was born + raised in Kansas - a real small town that I hated.

'X'-shaped letter K: when the letter 'k' is written with an 'x-shape' *(meaning if the letter stood alone you would think it was an 'x')* this indicates the writer has a complicated and potentially aggressive personality so others have a difficult time getting close to him.

Today is Monday, July 13, 2009 and I lost my job when 11 of us were laid off.

Corrugation: occurs when the stroke looks like corrugated cardboard. This indicates the writer has an authoritarian, and possibly brutal, personality. He lacks empathy and remorse. *This can be difficult to see without a magnifying glass. It is most common on vertical strokes.*

Many times my wife says that I am not a person who cares about others but I do.

Coiled 'o': vowels are *communication letters* so any disturbance in vowels indicates a disturbance in thoughts, body language, behaviors, etc. Therefore a coiled 'o' means the writer is narcissistic, stubborn, neurotic, may be psychotic and act under-handed.

Take my money, take my kids but don't Take my dog! You won't get no child #!!

Convex or downward t-crossings: if they look like mushroom top and / or cross downward toward the lower right then the writer is an authoritarian individual and likes to be in control so much that he can lack respect for others. *Also see "weapons or x's" in this section if the t-crossing causes the letter to look like the letter x if it stood alone.*

Tom and I are not ready To move but we are getting evicted because we both lost our jobs !!!!!! This sucks !!!!!!

Launching t-crossing: these t-crossings look like they are going to fly off the paper. This indicates a writer who can "fly off the handle" or is easily angered, has a hot temper, and can have outbursts of irrepressible rage. He can be a brutal enemy without warning.

CALL ME WHEN YOU ARRIVE DO NOT LEAVE YOUR PRIVATE

Clubbed endstrokes: in 90% of the population the exit stroke of letters get lighter and / or taper off. But the other 10% show an endstroke where the ink gets thicker or heavier at the very end. This indicates a writer who can display unexpected brutality. *Note that most of the pressure is seen at the exit stroke of the letters.*

I love flying Kites, mini Kites, and drinking coke and Brisk tea.

"Go to Hell K": when the lowercase 'k' is too large in comparison to the rest of the letters around it, it indicates the writer's defiance toward others. He can be especially challenging to authority figures.

Wednesday, May 16, law enforcement personnel, acting on a tip from one of our interviews, set up surveillance outside a blue house covered in ivy.

Downward entrance stroke: can be seen when the entrance of a letter enters the rest of the letter with a high and downward slant. The writer can be condescending and patronizing. He often has an unjustifiably high opinion of himself while demonstrating disdain for others whom he feels are 'less than' him.

My daughter is Julie and she can be quite the challenge!

I really love Jayme even if we fight a lot. She is supposed to be my wife whether anyone likes it or not.

'V'-shaped exit strokes: when the exit stroke of the lower loop makes a v-shape instead of a loop the writer can be physically aggressive. If you see this stroke only on an identifying word such as "daughter" or, *as seen in the above sample,* "Jayme" this indicates a potential victim.

Maybe they will let us go to the movie tonite but am not sure if he'll have money by then.

Initial horizontal stroke: when the entrance stroke is horizontal and leads into the rest of the letter. The writer is critical and able to find fault without reason

18

Your parents and grandparents probably learned a style like this with extended beginning and ending strokes. It slants and has very fancy capitals.

Closed or near-closed loops: anytime you see closed loops (especially lower) the writer tends to be anti-social and does not let just anyone know the real him.

Little accomplishments mean alot to a kid who does not do that well in School.

Break-away entrance stroke: when the entrance stroke separates from the rest of the letter it indicates the writer can be argumentative, stubborn and impulsive. Most commonly seen on letters *h, k, m, n, p.*

I gRaduaTed coLLege foR graPhic deSign anD am exciTed to geT my fiRsr joB.

Capitals in the middle of lowercase: if this occurs in 80% or more of his writing, the writer can become psychotic and sociopathic.

I am in school - college working toward my degree in international relationships + I know 3 languages that will help me land a good job I hope!

"Felon's claws" are regressive angles in the lower loops: Notice the claw shape in place of the lower loop. This represents a side of the writer that is resentful, vengeful, and who can deviantly manipulate others and then 'stab' them in the back when they least expect it. He can easily show spiteful hate to those who cross him and can be a ruthless and bitter enemy. *Note how often this stroke is seen in gang graffiti or tagging on both numbers and letters.*

Hey Spike,

This is Tim. Hows things going out thar
Tell every one I said Hi. And Hold my stuff
ok, I'll be back out in Febuary 07,
This person is my ex cellie And my new pop
man I sent Him to you to see if you Like
His stuff, I'll see you in a Few yeer Bro

Wavy baseline: when some words go up and some go down, this indicates the writer's moodiness. He can be immature with unpredictable thoughts and behaviors. He may not always be realistic and may spend a lot of time in a fantasy world. The last two lines are drawn under so you can see how they rise and fall. The more words that do this, the more moody the writer is.

How could You let this happen ?! Maybe you can
fix it so Nobodzy Renows about it !
                    Mitchell R.

Downward hook entrance stroke: when you see an entrance stroke that forms a 'v' inside the entrance loop this indicates a writer who can harass others in a condescending, derogatory manner. He can get joy out of harassing others that are at his mercy.

My goal is to move to Florida in
about November and hopefully
find a good job.

"Stinger" – a double entrance curve: this entrance stroke looks like the stinger of a hornet. The writer can be insincere and misrepresents or evade the truth. He can easily pretend to be what he isn't and will often hide his real intentions from others. Because of this he can be devious and lack morals. Many times their behaviors are aimed at the opposite gender but, if the opportunity isn't around, they don't discriminate.

Me and my boyfriend are excited to have a Baby.

Tight initial loops on entrance: when you see small or tight rolls on entrances or exits of letters, the writer can be very possessive and jealous and, if he feels there is a rival, can show intense and unrealistic expressions of emotion such as anger or manipulative tears.

My life has been full of trauma and drama and when I think things are going to get better - they do. Thats amazing.

Excessive 'tick' marks: these appear on the entrances or exits of letters and are little lines or hooks. These indicate misdirected and untreated anger issues. He may deny his anger but it may be the root of "evil" behavior and hostile outbursts or a disturbed self-identity.

Anyone who does not believe me can go to hell and never come back. I am telling the truth. I have no reason to lie.

Liar loops: remembering that vowels are communication letters, any time excessive loops show on vowels, the writer can be very deceptive and deliberately deceive or mislead others to hide his real intentions.

I am sorry we argued but I was right about it and you will realize soon enough and you will apologize to me. I don't need your apology but think you will want to give me one!

Rigid angled entrance: this is seen when it looks like the entrance is a bicycle's kickstand or when the letter looks as though it would tip over without that stroke. The writer can be resistant, habitually rebellious and, if contradicted, stubborn and antagonistic. If it starts under the word it forms resentment such as the following example.

resentment   happy

Resentment: With this stroke the circled section is unnecessary for the letter shape so it therefore means this writer is resentful over something from his past. To find out when it took place you will measure just the section that hangs below the rest of the word with a millimeter ruler. Each mm = 1 year back in the writers past. This stroke will only be on the left of the letter.

don't you want to go ? Let me know.

Maybe we don't need to be best friends if you are going to be like that. Jerk !

Wide 't' or 'd' loops: when the loops of these two letters are wide instead of closed, the writer is overly sensitive to criticism and fears rejection. When he feels unjustifiably hurt (even if there is no reason) he can show vicious sarcasm, resentment and aggression.

I am happy for you and today is the perfect day to announce your engagement

Tapered t-bars: sarcastic; inclined to make cutting remarks; can be destructive and violent

it really is not a good feeling to feel like this as you can imagine. Ive dealt with this feeling my whole life.

Exit strokes that go back over words: when exit strokes go leftward and start to go back over the word, the writer suffers from excessive guilt, self-blame and may even seek self-punishment. Even if it means hurting another individual and then becoming arrested, the arrest is the self-punishment.

The quick brown fox jumps over the lazy dog.

Super heavy pressure: the more heavy the pressure or the more the paper feels like Braille on the back, the more aggressive and forceful he is feeling. If it partially rips the paper then he can be a ruthless and heartless enemy.

will Cook AND FeeD anyonE motOWN FoOD

Letters progressively increase: note the letter size increase toward the right. The writer can be verbally blunt without tact or diplomacy and his social skills are typically under-developed. He suffers from feelings of inferiority and, to make up for it, his attitude indicates someone who can be psychologically unstable while easily and quickly losing control. Those that know him can attest to his often forceful expression of emotions and how he always likes the last word.

Many times I felt life has been unfair to me for no reason!

Strokes below the baseline: May indicate hidden aggression or sneaky thoughts or behaviors. He can act covert, subtle, or indirect and this indicates unpleasant subconscious urges and desires. These urges and desires may not be expressed or acknowledged openly, and therefore actions are likely to be hidden and subversive.

* plant trees?
* pull board + stove 'em
* vacuum car
* turn over garden
* bike x 2
* office she-yit
* storms
* ~~~~~~~
* ~~~~~~~
~ ~~~~~~~

Irregular pressure: some letters are darker and some are lighter throughout the sample. This is called inconsistent, misplaced, or irregular pressure and indicates a writer who can forcefully show his emotions. He may lack the ability to behave "normally" within society and his behaviors (including sexual) can be very violent.

Made my crew do extra work today because they were acting up on tuesday. They have time to make up for today.

Braced t or d's: the upside-down v-shape in the letters *d* and *l* or *t* indicates the writer is very stubborn. Alone this is not always negative however, if combined with other signs in this section, it usually is.

Once upon a Childhood Memory, I lo...
pedal sewing Machine that Mama sewed o...
This particular time Mama was Making me a...
the first day.
Mama was always singing songs to us a...
Mama sewed my little Coat of green, tol...
me the story of Joseph and the Coat's...
would always cry when Mama told the...
Joseph betrayed him and sold him into...
green my favorite from the Bible and th...
for me just Made me love the story...
the Coat that Mama was Making, was...

I think we have potential.
Would like to spend time with
you & have a relationship grow!
Yes, you think so?

Extreme right slant: What happens when <u>you</u> have a very emotional day? Your logic and objectivity becomes less and less powerful right. Therefore, the more right slanted your writing, the more the writer reacts emotionally and not logically which makes him prone to losing control.

I'm confused. I have mixed
feelings about Zac. I still have feelings
for Frank even though I know
he'll never go back out with me. I
can't get over him. Help before I
ruin my realisonship with Zac!
But I also like Scott in my
large class. Help.

Bizarre formations: this occurs when a letter, if it stood on its own, is unrecognizable or looks like a different letter. The example above shows several of these letters that represent the writer's unusual thinking style. This can indicate pathological obsessions which mean that the individual's thinking, philosophy, and/or behaviors may be altered to serve his own needs.

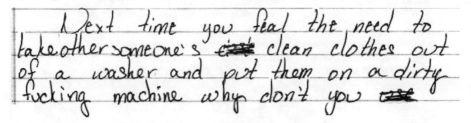

Excessively tall upper stems or loops: when the upper heights of the stems are too tall this indicates the writer has an unrealistic estimation of his self-worth and abilities. He expects praise and recognition – even if it is undeserved. He feels the rules do not apply to him. He may act vain, pompous, grandiose, narcissistic, etc. However he may even criticize others so he can look better than them.

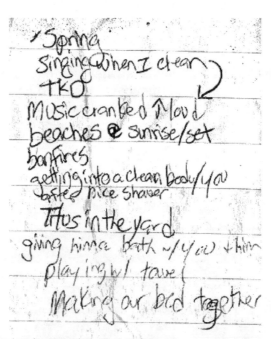

Erratic middle zone or lowercase size: if you focus just on the vowels it is easier to see the erratic sizes. This indicates that the writer is hyper-sensitive due to an unstable self-image. Because of this his responses depend on the circumstances. If he has a criminal intent, his crimes will be unpredictable.

Next time I see Mary I will ask her when she will be over here to pick up her pet rabbit. Yes my dear!

NBC
30 Rockefeller Ave
New York, NY

Weapons or X's: If **weapon** shapes appear it is an indicator that the writer could hurt someone (including himself). If you see pitchfork formations like the "Devil's Fork" the writer has something in common with Ted Bundy, Seung Hui-Cho, Dennis Rader, and Keith Jesperson who equally who showed no remorse for their crimes because the "devil made them do it". If there are random **x-shapes** (letter x does not count) it indicates an obsession with death or the ability to use weapons inappropriately. Either way, the writer has strong mental energy and, when combined with his physical drive, can lead to physical aggression. If it only appears on a specific individual's name, it is usually physical aggression aimed at that specific person. *Turn upside-down to find more because, if a stroke looks like it could hurt you – the writer can!*

happyness belongs to the person who wants to be happy but if some people don't want or feel they deserve happyness it really don't matter what anyone tries to tell them beap they won't listen anyway!!

Excessive tangling lines: whenever the lower loops tangle with the words or letter below, the writer is experiencing psychological confusion and may be incapable of clear and / or realistic thoughts.

not ⇩ sure ⇩ how ⇩ much ⇩ they ⇩ will ⇩ offer me for my car but they will get a good deal cuz my car is a great car and I am only selling it cuz I need money.

Rivers: rivers occur when the spacing between the words flow, like a river, all the way to the bottom. The more of these present, the more easily the writer can commit a crime without hesitation or true remorse. Most of the time this writer's crimes are heinous and violent. Note the arrows above. You can follow them all the way through to the bottom. The more that appear, the more violent an individual can be. Highlight them and see if they flow to or from one word or section of words. Those words may tell details or be symbolic of a crime.

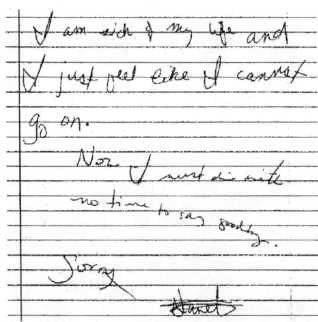

I am sick of my life and I just feel like I cannot go on. Now I must die with no time to say goodbye. Sorry

Lacking boundaries – if there is little or no regard for the lines on the paper then the writer feels that rules are made to be broken. These can be moral, societal, ethical or legal rules as he does not usually discriminate.

mother to let me know

Passive Aggressive – when the entrance stroke starts leftward and other letters are vertical or rightward. This writer shows can commit acts of obstructive resistance to anything he expected to complete. He may show you negative attitudes with passive denial, refusal or resistance in both personal and professional settings. Some behaviors that you will most frequently see include learned helplessness, procrastination, stubbornness, resentment, bad temper or hostility, the "silent treatment", refusal to be social or cooperate cheerfully, and deliberately being late, forgetful, or irresponsible. He may have a fear of intimacy, or have difficultly trusting others which both act as a barrier to emotional attachment. He may cause chaotic situations, make excuses for not being a team-player, or blame others for his failures to avoid having to face his own weaknesses. Even if he only has a couple of these behavior patterns he can still have non-passive-aggressive personality traits which make it difficult to recognize. However his emotions have been repressed due to a severe need for acceptance.

Falling apart - is indicated by lack of harmony, connections, stability, or any kind of consistency. This can happen over days, weeks, months or years. It is important to keep an eye on the writing to be sure. This trait indicates that the individual is feeling a physical or psychological breakdown. His thoughts, emotions and/or behavior are falling apart. This may be indicative of psychotic episodes.

29

LEARNING CHALLENGE: See which written indicators (other than those indicated below each sample) you can spot in the other handwriting samples.

This section will reveal the handwriting of some of the most horrific serial killers - most of whom brutally abused their victims.

Challenge yourself to see how many of the previous indicators you can locate in each of the handwriting samples that follow.

You mention that Stephen King said he talked to me on a TV show. He must mean in letters as I have written him in Maine. I also am a big fan of his Books and movies.

So No I have never met him. Dennis Hopper is an interesting actor + Director I think he would be an interesting man too.

Regards, John

I think it ridiculous to comment on it. Everything is written for the gullible Public who seem to love all that sensationalism, Sex, and gore, with know interests in knowing the True story.

regards,

John Wayne Gacy

John Gacy

J.W. Gacy
John W. Gacy

John Wayne Gacy – a serial killer who was active between 1972 and 1978. Before his arrest, he raped and murdered at least 33 boys and young men and boys with a preference for teenagers. Most of these victims (26) were buried underneath his house, the others were found in the Des Plaines River or elsewhere on his property. His nickname was the "Killer Clown" due to his charitable services at fundraising & children's events where he dressed up as "Pogo the Clown".

Dear Mr. LaFalce,

Recently, I saw an article in the Buffalo News that detailed a man's arrest; one of the charges being "possession of a noxious substance" (CS gas). This struck my curiosity, so, I went to the New York State Penal Law. Sure enough, section 270 prohibits possession of any noxious substance, and included in section 265 is a ban on the use of "stun guns". Now I am a male, and fully capable of physically defending myself, but how about a female?

I strongly believe in a God-given right to self-defense. Should any other person or a governing body be able to tell another person that he/she cannot save their own life, because it would be a violation of a law? In this case, which is more important: faced with a rapist/murderer, would you pick to a.) die, a law-abiding citizen or b.) live, and go to jail?

It is a lie if we tell ourselves that the police can protect us everywhere, at all times. I am in shock that a law exists which denies a woman's right to self-defense. Firearms restrictions are bad enough, but now a woman can't even carry mace in her purse?!?!.

TIM McVEIGH
6280 CAMPBELL BLVD
LOCKPORT, NY 14094

Timothy McVeigh - an U.S. Army veteran and former security guard who was convicted of detonating a truck bomb by the Alfred P. Murrah building in Oklahoma City in April 1995 which killed 168 people. Until September 11, 2001 this was the deadliest act of terrorism within the United States. McVeigh was a militia movement follower and had a goal of revenge against the federal government for the Waco Siege (where 76 people died exactly two years earlier) and wanted to incite a revolt against what he considered to be a tyrannical federal government.

FACTUAL STATEMENT
IN SUPPORT OF PLEA PETITION

On December 15th and 16th I rode with Tim McVeigh from my home in Kingman, Az. to Kansas. There I was to receive weapons that Tim McVeigh told me had been stolen by Terry Nichols, and himself. While in Kansas, McVeigh and I loaded about twenty-five weapons into a car that I had rented. On December 17th, 1994, I drove the rental car back to Arizona through Oklahoma and Oklahoma City. Later, after returning to Arizona and at the request of Tim McVeigh, I sold some of the weapons and again at the request of Tim McVeigh I gave him some money to give to Terry Nichols.

Prior to April 1995, McVeigh told me about the plans that he and Terry Nichols had to blow up the Federal Building in Oklahoma City, Oklahoma. I did not as soon as possible make known my knowledge of the McVeigh and Nichols plot to any judge or other persons in civil authority. When FBI agents questioned me later, about two days after the bombing, and during the next three days, I lied about my knowledge and concealed information. For example, I falsely stated that I had no knowledge of plans to bomb the federal building. I also gave certain items that I had received from McVeigh, including a bag of ammonium nitrate fertilizer, to a neighbor of mine so the items would not be found by law enforcement officers in a search of my residence.

Michael Joseph Fortier

Michael Fortier's above sample is a confession of his complicity in the Oklahoma City bombing *(see Timothy McVeigh on previous page)*. After signing this plea agreement with prosecutors, he testified before a grand jury for almost four hours. He pled guilty to conspiring to transport stolen guns, lying to FBI agents, and concealing his knowledge of the plot. He was sentenced after testifying at the McVeigh trial.

There is a demon inside my soul. It has always been there. My demon tries to lead me down paths I do not want to follow. At times that demon has lured me into doing things I did not want to do.

For almost 40 years God has been struggling with my demon, and eventually God always prevailed. My demon is working inside my soul again, filling me with despair and taking away my hope. My demon has finally gotten the upper hand.

All my life people have seen me as strong. The truth is just the opposite. I am the weakest of the weak. People have seen me as good. The truth is just the opposite. I am the baddest of the bad. People have seen me as virtuous. The truth is just the opposite. I am the lowest of the low.

Walker L. Railey

Walker Railey – the head minister of First United Methodist Church who was acquitted (because there were no witnesses and no physical evidence) for the strangulation of his wife in the garage of their comfortable Dallas home. In the near fatal attack, her windpipe was crushed and her brain was without oxygen for more than two hours as she lay on the garage floor. She exists now in what her doctors call a "constant vegetative state" not knowing how much she sees, hears, does or does not feel.

When I left my home on Tuesday, October 25, I was very emotionally distraught. I didn't want to live anymore! I felt like things could never get any worse. When I left home, I was going to ride around a little while and then go to my mom's. As I rode and rode and rode, I felt even more anxious coming upon me about not wanting to live. I felt I couldn't be a good mom anymore but I didn't want my children to grow up without a mom. I felt I had to end our lives to protect us all from any grief or harm ████████████████ I had never felt so lonely and so sad in my entire life. I was in love with someone very much, but he didn't love me and never would. I had a very difficult time accepting that. But I had hurt him very much and I could see why he could never be me. When I was @ John D. Long lake, ██████ I had never felt so scared and unsure as I did then. I wanted to end my life so bad and was in my car ready to go down that ramp into the water and I did go part way, but I stopped. I went again and stopped. I then got out of the car and stood by the car a nervous wreck. Why was I feeling this way? Why was everything so bad in my life? I had no answers to these questions. I dropped to the lowest when I allowed my children to go down that ramp into the water without me. I took off running and screaming, "Oh God! Oh God, No! What

---

The above sample, as well as the one that follows, were written by **Susan Smith** – who was sentenced to life in prison for murdering her two sons, 3-year-old Michael Daniel Smith, and 14-month-old Alexander Tyler Smith. She stated she suffered from mental health issues that impaired her judgment. According to the South Carolina Department of Corrections, Smith will be eligible for parole on November 4, 2024, after serving a minimum of thirty years. She is most recently incarcerated in the South Carolina Leath Correctional Institution but, since her incarceration, two guards have been punished for having sex with her.

I knew from day one, the truth would prevail but I was so scared I didn't know what to do. It was very tough emotionally to sit and watch my family hurt like they did. It was time to bring a peace of mind to everyone, including myself. My children deserve to have the best and now they will. I broke down on Thursday, November 3 and told Sheriff Howard Wells the truth. It wasn't easy, but after the truth was out, I felt like the world was lifted off my shoulders. I know now that it is going to be a tough and long road ahead of me. At this very moment, I don't feel I will be able to handle what's coming, but I have prayed to God that he give me the strength to survive each day and to face those times and situations in my life that will be extremely painful. I have put my total faith in God and he will take care of me.

Susan V. Smith
11/3/94
5:05 p.m.

The above sample is a confession written by **Susan Smith**. See previous page for her story.

However, I am not one to cry out a case of injustice.

I hope Mayor Beame enjoys dribbling my head across the court. This is really like a circus event with clowns and criminals. Please bring a beer when you come.

Sincerely,
David Berkowitz

David Berkowitz - known as "Son of Sam" and the ".44 Caliber Killer" terrorized residents in New York City from 1976 until his arrest in 1977. After his arrest he confessed to killing six people and wounding seven others. He claimed he was commanded to kill a neighbor's dog that was possessed by a demon. He then said he lied about his original confession and only killed three people. He said the other victims were killed by members of a violent Satanic cult that he was a member of. David was the only person charged in the shootings but authorities believe that many members of the cult were responsible for committing the murders. This case was reopened in 1996 and, as of 2004, it still was.

Glen Rogers 124400
FLORIDA STATE PRISON
P.O. BOX 181
STARKE, FL, 32091

Glen Rogers - the "Cross-Country Killer" who was a charming, handsome and volatile individual that went on a cross-country rampage that left four women dead in various states. A womanizer, his hobby was to pick up blond and redheaded women in a bar and give them rides home where the killings came as a drunken afterthought. He is considered a "spree killer" who, unlike serial killers, do not have "cooling off periods" between victims. Glen killed with his randomly sudden bursts of rage erupted. Prior to his arrest he worked as a construction worker and had numerous run-ins with authorities. On at least one occasion when police arrived at his house for a domestic violence call, Glen poked a lit blowtorch through the peephole. Authorities believe he may have killed twelve people but, two days prior to his arrest, he told his sister that he killed more than 70 women.

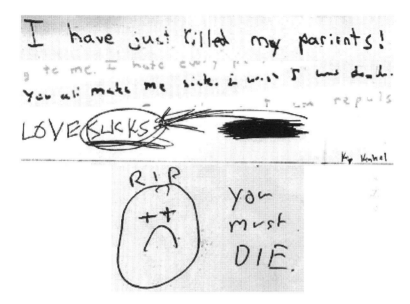

Kip Kinkel – the Oregon school shooter who killed his parents the day before. At the age of 15, he murdered his parents in May 1998, and the next morning engaged in a school shooting at Thurston High School in Springfield, Oregon. Two students died and 22 others were wounded. He is serving a 111-year sentence, without the possibility of parole.

DID YOU KNOW ?

That learning to write cursive at a young age creates and builds empathy and remains with us as an adult even if we do not continue cursive writing styles. **Kip Kinkel** is just one of the kids who started school in Spain at the age of 6. It is believed he did not learn to write cursive *(as in many other countries that stopped teaching cursive 30+ years ago)*. When he returned to Oregon his teachers stated he "lacked emotional development for his age". Unempathetic kids turn into violent teens and adults yet we wonder why societal violence worsens almost daily! Now the USA has stopped most handwriting classes too! **Join me** to bring cursive back to elementary schools globally. **Ask me how!**

Earlier, I sent several news items to this Court in Appellant's First and Second Letters to the Court Respecting Victims' Assertion of Privacy Rights. In Named Victims' Brief, at 53, Mr. Hirsch complained that in so doing I "fail[ed] to comply with Federal Rule of Appellate Procedure 10(e)". I'm not sure that this is correct, since it would seem that my action was justified by Rule 10(e)(3): I "presented to the court of appeals" the question of what to do with the information I offered. Moreover, the Court can take judicial notice of some information that does not appear in the record.

Anyway, if the Court feels I am acting improperly in sending it Exhibits A and B, then obviously the Court is free to disregard those exhibits.

Dated: Respectfully submitted,

July 15, 2008 *Theodore John Kaczynski*

   THEODORE JOHN KACZYNSKI

Ted Kaczynski - Dr. Theodore John Kaczynski is mostly known as the "Unabomber" was a mathematician and social critic who engaged in a mail bombing spree that lasted approximately 20 years while killing three and injuring 23 people. As a very intelligent child and teen he was accepted into Harvard University at the age of 16 and eventually obtained his PhD in Mathematics from the University of Michigan. He worked for a short time as an assistant professor at the University of California in Berkeley. In 1971 he moved to a remote cabin without electricity or running water in Montana where he self-taught self-sufficiency and wilderness survival skills. He then launched his personal bombing campaign because he disliked seeing the wilderness around his home get destroyed by development. During the years of 1978 to 1995 he sent 16 bombs to targets including universities and airlines. He admitted his bombings were extreme but necessary to stop the erosion of human freedom via modern technologies and large-scale organizations. To-date he is one of the FBI's most expensive investigations. He was not caught due to evidence or investigations by the authorities, he was caught because of his brother who recognized Ted's style of writing and beliefs from the manifesto, and tipped off the FBI.

walk in, set bombs at 11:09 for 11:17
leave, set bombs.
Drive to designate park. Clean up.
Get back by 11:15
Park cars, set car bombs for 11:18
get out. go to outside hill, wait.
when first bombs go off, attack.
have fun!

Written by one of the **Columbine school shooters** - the Columbine High School massacre occurred on Tuesday, April 20, 1999, just outside of Littleton, Colorado. Two senior students, Eric Harris and Dylan Klebold, embarked on a massacre, killing 12 students and one teacher. Their actions injured 21 other students directly, and three people were injured while attempting to escape. They then committed suicide. It is the fourth-deadliest school massacre in United States history, after the 1927 Bath School disaster, 2007 Virginia Tech massacre and the 1966 University of Texas massacre, and the deadliest for an American high school.

☐ YES ☐ NO Do you feel your creative juices because the mouth at least twice a week through no fault of your own?

☐ YES ☐ NO Do you find yourself spelling "frustration" with a capital F, while also dotting the i and carefully crossing both t's?

If 5 of the 9 questions are in the obvious negative, not merely assumed, then you know the obvious answer.

There are many people who unfortunately deserve this and others who actually thrive on this here. The ability to independantly put one foot in front of the other, smile and read out warmly keeps you out of the county mainstream here. I'm hoping that your intelligence and abilities will cause you to make a successful judgement and move in to greener pastures.

Best sincerely,

Ken

Kenneth Alessio Bianchi – the serial killer who, with his cousin Angelo Buono, Jr. were known as the "Hillside Stranglers". Bianchi is also a suspect in the Alphabet murders which took place in New York where three young girls were raped and strangled and each girl had matching first and last name initials, and whose bodies were found in a town that started with the same letter as the girls' names.

Eric,   23 Mar. 1993

Hey there guy. Well... I'm grabbling
for your hand now my friend.
First things first: I was told the
same thing. Once you renounce Jesus you can't
ever go back. That's garbage. I've ...
I've been a Christian now for 10 years. When
you reach out to God He forgives.
God said: "Again, when I say to the
wicked, 'You shall surely die,' if he turns from
his sin and does what is lawful and right, if the
wicked restores the pledge, gives back what he
has stolen, and walks in the statutes of life without
committing iniquity, he shall surely live; he shall
not die. None of his sins which he has committed
shall be remembered against him; he has done
what is lawful and right, he shall surely live."
                    - Ezekiel 33: 14 - 16
Here's what you're going to have to do
Eric. You're going to have to live your life.
for God. Not for yourself, not for your
family, but for God. You have to give
yourself to Him body and soul. You were

Sean Seller – the 16-year-old who first killed Robert Bower, a convenience store clerk in Oklahoma because Bower refused to sell him beer and because Seller wanted to see "what it felt like". A few months late, on March 5, 1986, he killed his mother and step-father while they were sleeping. He tried to arrange the crime scene to look as if an intruder had committed the killings as an effort to hide his guilt. He stated that he read The Satanic Bible by Anton Lavey "hundreds of times" between the ages of 15 and 16 and, at the time that the crimes were committed, he was possessed by a demon and therefore not guilty of his crimes.

43

— you feel like your thoughts push you outside of any possible friendship with someone who doesn't always agree with you ... as I said, relax.

You could have 20 tattoos, a double mastectomy and purple hair - hang by your feet in a casket at night and dream of really unusual things — so? So what?

Be Good D. Clark

Douglas Clark, along with Carol Bundy *(see next page),* are known as the "Sunset Strip Killers". They were convicted of a series of killings in Los Angeles. Previous to the killings, Clark held regular blue collar jobs but was fired due to threats of violence against co-workers. He later met and moved in with Carol Bundy. The relationship quickly became abusive with Clark paying less and less attention to her. Desperate for time with him, Clark started sharing his violent fantasies with Bundy, and in June 1980, they committed their first murder. The majority of the duo's victims were prostitutes that Clark killed during intercourse. Clark stated he always had fantasies of killing a woman during intercourse and feeling her vaginal contractions during the death spasms. Clark and Bundy would lure the victim into their car and the victim would then be forced to perform fellatio on Clark. Bundy would then place a gun into Clark's open palm, and he would shoot the victim in the back of the head. On at least one occasion they saved the head of a victim and stored it in a freezer to for use as a sex toy.

When you write me would
you please use something heavy
and dark to write with? Hate if my
eyes heal in legally blind and life
is a bitch!

I still haven't heard from the
court so I don't know anything new
there to tell you. Maybe next time
I'll have something interesting to
talk about

Take care, Eric, and stay

well

all my best.

Carol

This was written by **Carol Bundy**, along with Douglas Clark are known as the "Sunset Strip Killers. The story is on the previous page.

It is not believed that she is related to Ted Bundy (next page).

Think you for your letter of January 25, 1988, and for the documents you enclosed with it. I also received in a separate mailing your "Cartz-Clark Rose hypothesis."

There won't be any need to send me the other material I requested in my last letter. I appreciate your willingness to send it, but I think I have enough information to form an opinion concerning your allegations about Carol Bundy and the Winn Book.

What I intend to address in this letter are two topics: Carol's correspondence with me and the contention that she patterned the Sunset Strip murders upon information contained in a book by Steve Winn about Ted Bundy. As I understand it, you are interested in the letters Carol wrote me because they may bolster the Winn book connection in one way or

---

Ted Bundy - a very active serial killer between 1974 and 1978. Although nobody knows precisely how many murders he committed, he did confess to 30. However, authorities have estimated as many as 100. He seemed to vent his rage on mostly college girls while keeping the perfect image of a normal, intelligent, and model citizen. He beat his victims, strangled them, and was very well practiced necrophilia. The numbers attributed to him are difficult to confirm because of his interstate travels and the clever ways he disposed of evidence. One thing authorities have confirmed is that he has been one of the most prolific and frightening serial killers of all time.

During my stay at CCC, I have had a chance to look at my life from an angle that was never presented to me before. What I did was deplorable. The world has enough misery in it without my adding more to it. Sir, I can assure you that it will never happen again. This is why, Judge Gardner, I am requesting from you, a sentence modification. So that I may be allowed to continue my life as a productive member of our society.

Respectfully Yours,
Jeff Dahmer

Jeffrey Dahmer - serial killer and sex offender who murdered 17 men and boys of which most were African or Asian. As a child and teen he biked around his neighborhood looking for dead animals, which he dissected at home, and even put a dog's head on a stake. His murders involved rape, torture, dismemberment, cannibalism, and necrophilia. On November 28, 1994, he was beaten to death by an inmate at the Columbia Correctional Institution, where he was incarcerated for these crimes.

're ... I'...
time. ...
h and every day of ...

Your Loving Friend
+ Brother in Christ
Bill

Bill Bonin
P.O. Box C-44600
4-E-62
Tamal, Ca. 94974

Bill Bonin - a serial killer once referred to as the "Freeway Killer" (however there have been 3 different serial killers with that nickname) was also a twice-paroled sex offender. Between 1979 and 1980 he tortured, raped and killed at least 21 boys and young men but authorities feel he is responsible for up to 35. Bonin typically chose young male hitchhikers, schoolboys or male prostitutes as his victims of which all were between the ages of 12 and 19. Once in Bonin's van they were overpowered, bound with their hands behind their back, sexually assaulted, tortured and then killed. Usually he strangled his victims with their own t-shirt but some were stabbed or battered to death. At least one victim was forced to drink Chlorohydrate Acid, two other victims had ice-picks driven into their ears, and at least victim died of shock. Once dead, their bodies were discarded alongside various southern Californian freeways. Eventually Bonin was convicted and executed in 1996 for 14 of these murders.

PAGE:1 DATE MARCH - 18 - 2009

DEAR: NEW TEN NOW

I AM JIVERLY WONG SHOOTING THE PEOPLE

THE FIRST I WANT TO SAY SORRY I KNOW A LITTLE ENGLISH I HOPE YOU UNDERSTAND ALL OF THIS. OF COURSE YOU NEED TO KNOW WHY I SHOOTING? BECAUSE UNDERCOVER COP GAVE ME A LOT OF ASS DURING EIGHTEEN YEARS I GOT SEVEN YEARS AND EIGHT MONTH DELIVERY TO GROCERY IN THE CALIFORNIA CAME BACK NEW YORK ON THE AUGUST. 2007 LET TALK ABOUT WHEN I LIVE IN CALIFORNIA. SUCH AS...COP USED 24 HOURS THE TECHNIQUE OF ULTRAMODERN AND CAMERA FOR BURN THE CHEMICAL IN MY HOUSE. FOR SWITCH THE CHANNEL TIVI FOR ADJUST THE FAN. FOR MADE ME UNBREATHBLE. FOR MADE ME VOMIT. FOR CONNECT THE MUSIC INTO MY EAR.

UNDERCOVER COP USUAL COINED SOME NASTY WAS NOT TRUE ABOUT ME AND SPREAD A RUMOUA TO THE RECEIVER AND SOME PEOPLE KNOW ME CONDUCE TOWARD MANY PEOPLE PREJUDICED AND SET SELFISH TO ME... COP MADE ME LOST MY JOB... COP PUT ME BECAME POOR.

LET TALK ABOUT WHEN I LIVE AT THE 28. BAKER ST 2ND FLOOR. JOHNSON CITY NEW YORK. 13790. IT TERRIBLE WHEN I LIVE THERE SUCH AS... COP WAIT UNTIL MIDNIGHT WHEN I OFF THE LIGHT AND WENT TO THE BED. COP UNLOCK MY DOOR AND CAME IN TAKE A SIT IN MY ROOM << COP DID IT THIRTEEN TIME ON THE YEAR 1994 >> ON THE THIRTEEN TIME HAD THREE

Jiverly Wong – a naturalized immigrant who went into the American Civic Association in Binghamton, New York and started shooting. Fourteen people were confirmed dead, including Wong, and four were wounded. Most of the injured people were in the ESL classroom and ranged in age from twenty to mid-fifties and were treated and released. The American Civic Association in Binghamton provides citizenship, cultural, and language assistance to the local immigrant community.

Lewis Eugene Gilbert – he killed during his cross-country crime spree that began in Ohio in August 1994, and ended in Missouri. Gilbert was convicted and handed death sentences and life without parole and was ultimately executed.

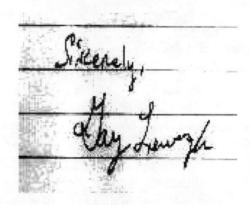

Gary Lewingdon, along with his brother Thadeus, were called the ".22 Caliber Killers" because, between February and December 1978, residents of Columbus, Ohio, lived in fear due to their random, senseless murders by way of nocturnal home invasions and numerous gunshots (at close range) to each residents head.

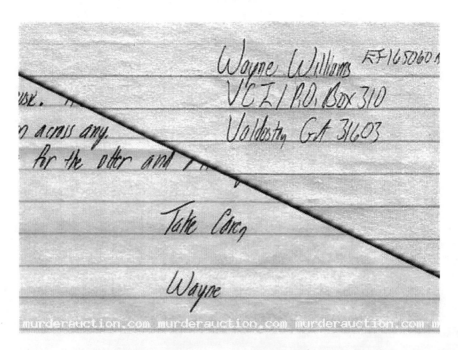

Wayne Bertram Williams - the "Atlanta Child Killer" whom authorities believe killed approximately 29 children from 1979 until 1981. He was convicted of murdering two adult men. After his conviction, the Atlanta police declared the "Atlanta Child Murders" case was solved and closed with Williams shown to be the killer.

Seung-Hui Cho – the senior undergraduate student who started shooting at the Virginia Polytechnic Institute and State University (known as the Virginia Tech Massacre). His rampage took the lives of 32 people and wounded 25 others. Cho committed suicide when law enforcement officers were near apprehension.

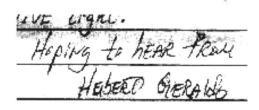

Hubert Geralds - was charged with six homicides of prostitutes and female drug-addicts in 1995. However, another individual has recently confessed to the murders and most recently his convictions are pending a new trial.

Homemade B.B.Q. or Spegetti Sauce
1-Cup Blood
½ can. tomato puree or paste.
2 cloves of garlic
1½ tsp. salt
1-Cup fresh Jallapeno peppers
½ Cup mushrooms
⅙ Cup vinegar
Cook tomato puree o paste to a slow simmer on low flame
or heat up to 15 minutes. Blood, Jallapeno peppers, mushrooms
and cloves of garlic together and mix with vinegar and salt,
when tomato puree/paste begins to simmer mix all together
and cook for 5 minutes for thick sauce. For spegetti sauce
exclude vinegar. Good for 4 to 6 servings of meat and
spegetti.

Ottis Elwood Toole

Ottis Elwood Toole – an accomplice of convicted serial killer Henry
Lee Lucas *(see below).* Toole admitted to multiple acts of murder,
rape, and cannibalism. He was also the suspect in several unsolved
murders but was convicted of three and, prior to his death while in
prison, confessed to four more. Toole is also the one who took the life
of little Adam Walsh (son of John Walsh, America's Most Wanted).

Henry Lee Lucas

Henry Lee Lucas - convicted of multiple murders and once listed as
America's most prolific serial killer. Lucas confessed to involvement in
about 600 murders yet claimed to a researched, *"I am not a serial
killer".* He claimed his murders averaged one every five days between
mid-1975 to his re-arrest in mid-1983. His cohort was Ottis Elwood
Toole *(see above).*

All the way out the alley to E. Chesterfield Street.

Are you willing to expose the fact that Foy lied about the car he saw in the alley that night and its color.

Are you willing to expose the fact that the Attorney General's office hid or distroyed photographs of the crime scene. And lost the cast made of tire tracks in the snow.

I can show you the big lie from beginning to end from the evidance and how it was carryed out.

The unperverted truth! Without all the twisting to make the pieses fit.

I know you are willing to burn my ass at the stake and print whatever lie, half truth, tell is told about me, but are you will to do the same to the Attorney General's office about the lies they have been telling on me in the Dutcher and Stell cases.

well that all for now

Coral Watts

Coral Eugene Watts - nicknamed Coral, a serial killer called "The Sunday Morning Slasher". Authorities suspect that he has killed more than 100 women but he obtained immunity for a dozen murders as a result of a 1982 plea bargain. He was set to be released in 2006 but died of prostate cancer while serving two life sentences without parole in a Michigan prison.

I pray whoever should read this will find it in
to forgive me. Round all, whoever you may be,
once a gentleman. May the good lord have mercy on.
forgive me for all I have done.

I give my name that all know of me, so history do
can do to a gentleman born.
　　　　Yours truly
　　　　Jack the Ripper
　　　　Dated this third day of May 1889.

6 Oct 1885

You though yourself very clever I reckon
when you informed the police But you
make a mistake if you though I dident
see you Now I know you know me and
I see your little game, and I mean
to finish you and send your ears to
your wife if you show this to the police
or helped them if you do I will finish
you. It is use your trying to get out
of my way Because I have you when
you dont expect it and I keep one
word as you soon see and rip you
up Yours truly Jack the Ripper

"Jack the Ripper" – the unidentified serial killer - active in the poorest areas of London in 1888. Other nicknames were "The White Chapel Murderer" and "Leather Apron". Victims were female prostitutes from the slums whose throats were cut then abdominally mutilated. The removal of internal organs of several of these victims led the authorities to believe that 'Jack' possessed knowledge in anatomy or surgery. Because of the excessive brutality of the murders, and the matching items between cases by the media, public acceptance has deemed this believed-to-be single serial killer "Jack the Ripper". We don't need to know the true identity of these writers because we can see that, even if they aren't the notorious "Jack the Ripper", they are still dangerous.

Have fun.

he Smile

Your Paul

Sincerely,
Paul Bateson

Paul Bateson - In 1977 and 1978, New York homosexuals were terrorized by the "Bag Murderer." Six male victims were mutilated and dismembered with their remains wrapped in black trash bags and dumped in the Hudson River. After police located bodies, they traced the recovered clothing to a shop in Greenwich Village known for distinctive tattoos and clothing that cater to homosexuals. Lacking identities and confirmed cause of death in several cases, the crimes were not officially classified as homicides. On September 14, 1977, in what seemed to be an "unrelated" case, film critic Addison Verrill was beaten and stabbed to death. Bateson, an X-ray technician, was charged with the slaying. He stated that, after having sex, he crushed Verrill's skull with a skillet, then stabbed Verrill in the heart. Bateson was convicted of the murder and sentenced to a term of 20 years to life. While incarcerated he bragged of killing other men "for fun," dismembering their bodies, and dropping the bagged remains in the Hudson River. Detectives were satisfied with Bateson's incarceration and he was never charged with the "bag murders".

The above sample, as well as the sample that follows, was written by **Sylvia Seegrist**. Sylvia opened fire at a mall in Springfield, Pennsylvania on Halloween and killed three people while wounding seven others. One of the victims was a two-year-old child. Sylvia was 25 years old and had been diagnosed with paranoid schizophrenia when she was 15 years old. Having been committed and discharged several times, her case stimulated discussion about the state's authority to remove individual rights of dangerous people in the interest of societal safety.

OK - [illegible]

This is what I write for the [illegible]

OK. (Communion wafers, rice, and bread, A million people in any ground, any any stadium, 2 cars and a grocery store every person, right? (about) statistically, any [illegible] any people in office buildings [illegible] [illegible]. Petrochemical products include gasoline, styrofoam (like cups) for meetings hospital stuff, too, plastic - plastic for toothbrushes, synthetic rubber, for hoses and carburetors in cars and aircraft and boat parts (fiberglass). Waxed paper - is for bread and milk cartons, plastic [illegible] for milk cartons, plastic wrap and wax paper, meat and bread. Paint is a petrochemical product - glue and [illegible] ink in pens [illegible] ink on newsprint [illegible] also clothes dyed, and [illegible] in television and [illegible] - so when it comes to meat and [illegible] - and bread for church - and [redacted] 2 cars and a grocery store every individual in a [illegible] I saw a [redacted] Seegrist [illegible] worried about [illegible] [illegible] [illegible] [illegible] Africa [illegible]

The above sample was written by **Sylvia Seegrist**. See her story and another handwriting sample on the previous page.

Richard Ramirez - known as the "Night Stalker" was a serial killer, sex offender and burglar. He was a satanic sensationalist and often drew the five-point pentagram on his body. During his trial, he would shout "Hail Satan!" in open court and his favorite song was "Night Prowler" by AC/DC. Ramírez was charged with 14 murders and 31 other felonies related to his 1985 spree. He was also charged with a 15th murder in San Francisco and a rape and attempted murder charge in Orange County. *The 'scribble' on his second sample above is intended to be a word… but what word ?*

Gerald Gallego, along with his wife, Charlene Adelle Gallego, were serial killers who terrorized Sacramento, California between 1978 and 1980. The first husband and wife serial killer team in the USA, they used charm, skill, and tricks to lure "sex slaves" to their deaths. Over a 26 month period, they kidnapped, sexually assaulted, bludgeoned, and murdered nine women (mostly teenagers) and one man in the Western United States. Once caught, they faced each other oppressively in a very memorable courtroom showdown.

Mr. C. Michael Gary

Carlton Gary - serial killer known as the "Stocking Strangler", he is alleged to have raped and / or murdered seven elderly woman between 1977-78 in Columbus, Georgia. He was convicted of beating, sexually assaulting and strangling the victims, mostly by using stockings. Two of the survivors testified that he strangled them into unconsciousness before raping or attempting to rape them. One Georgia survivor positively identified him as her attacker in court. Sometimes Carlton Gary would simply attack and kill his victims, but his modus operandi, was to rape and murder them. His oldest known victim was 10 days from her 90th birthday and his youngest was 55 years old. He was sentenced to life and lives on Death Row in Georgia.

Friends:

Robin

Robin Gecht - one of the "Ripper Crew" or "Chicago Rippers" which was a satanic cult composed of Gecht *(who once worked for serial killer John Wayne Gacy)* and three associates *(Edward Spreitzer with brothers Andrew and Thomas Kokoraleis)*. They were suspects in disappearances of 18 women in Chicago, Illinois. Gecht and his gang allegedly drove around looking for prostitutes to sacrifice in his apartment. They removed one breast from each victim and ate it as Robin read passages out of *The Satanic Bible*. After severing the breast, they each took turns raping the open wound and then each one took turns masturbating into the flesh of the breast. Then they chopped it into pieces and ate it. They were arrested in 1982 and Gecht is serving a 120 year sentence in the Menard Correctional Center.

Ed Gein - murderer and body snatcher. His crimes achieved widespread notoriety after authorities discovered Gein had exhumed corpses from local graveyards and created keepsakes from their bones and skin. When police arrested Gein after finding body parts in his house in 1957, he confessed to killing two women. He was tried in 1968 for the murder of one woman and sentenced to life imprisonment to be served in a mental ward. Robert H. Gollmar, the judge in the Gein case, wrote: "Due to prohibitive costs, Gein was tried for only one murder." With only two kills, Gein does not meet the traditional definition of a serial killer. However his life strongly influenced the creation of fictional serial killers such as *Leatherface* from <u>The Texas Chainsaw Massacre</u>. *Norman Bates* from <u>Psycho</u>, and *Jame Gumb* from <u>The Silence of the Lambs</u>.

David Gore - David Gore and his cousin, Freddie Waterfield, kidnapped two girls, aged 14 and 17 while they were hitchhiking in July 1983. They drove the girls back to Gore's house, took them to his bedroom, handcuffed them each, and then separated them. Gore cut the clothing off of one girl and sexually assaulted her three times. After Gore left her, she heard Gore tell the other girl that he would kill her if she did stay quiet. Gore then put the previous girl in a closet, where she heard a couple gunshots. When Gore returned, he put her in the attic, where she was later rescued by the police. A witness stated that she saw a naked girl run down the driveway of Gore's home, and Gore, also naked, was chasing after her. When Gore caught her, he threw her to the ground, dragged her to the tree and shot her in the head twice. Those are the shots her friend heard while in the closet.

Albert DeSalvo – the "Boston Strangler" who, at the age of 31 killed several elderly women followed by younger women. His victims were thirteen single women between the ages of 19 and 85. He would rape them and then strangle them with their own clothing. However his oldest victim actually died of a heart attack while two others were stabbed to death and one of them badly beaten. In his youth, he had an extensive history of trapping dogs and cats in boxes and shooting arrows through them. He was stabbed to death in prison in 1973.

citead each other wise)Tightly pure
herein divinely understanding
)he language indeed OF "Love"
(I) would fare once "Like")a Find
One decent and mature women
Trustworthy who has no Fear
herein "Love" to belly "Loved" and
Sharing OF her True emotions
and her Love: Herein the very
depths OF the soul and heart'
whom has been awaiting the
human Touch and such warmth
embrace OF this male:
whom is Standing with empty
Arm's awaiting)o be Filled:
Dream indeed a dream because
to Thice She'll be impossible:
When both are working "Together"
herein perfec) **harmony** Solely)o

Harrison Graham - convicted on seven counts of first-degree murder and seven counts of abusing a corpse. He was sentenced to life imprisonment, after six electrocutions which helped assure that he would never be granted parole. Another sample of his writing follows on the next page.

This institution has already [redacted]
Forced every Last One Of Us
without "Question" to send Our
Personal property "Home"
inmates will be provide RHU
Jumpsuit and Footwear !
which we were Given State brown
Clothing now we have these
RHU "Jumpsuits" personally within
reality its something you would

God watch Over you indeed
: From Harrison T. Graham .

Harrison Graham wrote the above sample. Read his story on the previous page.

Waldo Grant - a Georgia native, Grant fled a failed marriage by migrating to New York City in 1971, settling in a bachelor apartment on Manhattan's Upper West Side. Neighbors knew him as a quiet loner, with detectives furnishing descriptions of *"the kind of guy who lives in a tenement block for years, and nobody raises an eyebrow."* More to the point, no one suspected that Grant's secret hobby was murder. The first to die was 18-year-old Philip Mitchell, stabbed and bludgeoned with an iron bar on September 14, 1973, then hurled from the rooftop of Grant's apartment building in an effort to simulate suicide. Nearly two years elapsed before Grant struck again, stabbing 23-year-old George Muniz numerous times, and dumping his corpse in a trash bin, a few doors down from Grant's residence. Number three was Harold Phillips, age 30, hammered to death in his own apartment on October 3, 1976. On December 29 of that year, police found 16-year-old Harry Carrillo in Central Park, his body sawed into three pieces, wrapped in plastic bags, and left in a shopping basket. All four victims were described as homosexuals by homicide investigators. An acquaintance of Carrillo's, Grant was routinely questioned by police as part of their investigation, later singled out as a suspect on the basis of evidence found with the body. In custody, he confessed all four murders, citing an "uncontrollable urge" to kill in each case.

Inmate Name *Walter B. Kelbach*
Inmate Number *11867*
Housing Unit *Oquirrh 4*

Walter Kelbach – an ex-con who, with his cousin, lover and fellow ex-con Myron Lance, admitted they liked to get high on drugs and kidnap people. Once in the vehicle they drove them into the desert and forced them to sexual acts on them. They then sodomized and, when finished with the victim, would flip a coin to decide which of them would kill him. When Kelbach "won", he liked to repeatedly stab the victims and then toss their bodies into a roadside ditch. At least on one occasion then entered a bar and announced they were robbing the place. To prove to the patrons that they were serious, Lance shot a randomly-chosen older patron through the head. They continued to rob the place and fled but police arrested them at a roadblock. They were both charged with first-degree murder, and quickly the jury arrived at a guilty verdict and included the death sentence. About that time the Supreme Court set aside capital punishment and both were spared. Neither Kelbach or Lance ever expressed empathy or remorse – instead Lance coldly stated he *"don't have any feelings toward the victims"* and Kelbach stated, *"Yeah and I don't care about people getting hurt because I just like to watch."*

Sincerely,

Bobby Joe Long – (AKA: Bobbie Joe Long, Robert Joe Long and Robert Joseph Long). No matter what his alias, he is a serial killer who, as of October 2007, was on death row in Florida. Before Bobby moved to Florida, he lived in Long Beach, California and started contacting women through the Penny Saver. When he found women alone he would brutally rape, and rob them. Authorities never prosecuted him for these crimes. He then started answering classified ads for small appliances and, when he found women home alone, he raped them.

He was convicted for rape in 1981 but requested, and was given, a new trial in which the charges were dropped. In 1984 Long then relocated to Florida and committed at least 50 rapes in Fort Lauderdale and Miami areas. He was dubbed the "Classified Ad Rapist". Then, within eight months, he kidnapped, raped, and murdered 10 women in Tampa Bay. He raped his last victim for 26 hours then let her go. In 1985 he pled guilty to all of these receiving 26 life sentences without parole, seven life sentences with parole, and, through legal maneuvers, was given the electric chair.

Kevin Haley – along with his brother, the two kidnapped at least eight women (both young and elderly) and performed rape, sodomy, oral copulation, murder, and nearly everything between on their victims.

Gerald Eugene Stano – unattractive to nearly all who saw him, he considered himself the complete opposite dubbing himself as the "real Italian stallion". He may have been Italian but he wasn't a stallion – he was a cold-blooded psychopath who confessed to 33 gruesome murders. However authorities state the number is now at 41 because twenty-two of the bodies have been found and identified.

they are Able! I am the hatred in every man's heart! I am the epitome of all Evil! I have no mercy for humanity, for they created me, they tortured me until I snapped and became what I am today! My advice to any man who has been tortured by humanity is this: Let these words ring through our your heart, mind, and soul! Hate humanity! Hate humanities say: Hate what humanity has made you! Hate what you have become! Most of all, hate the accursed god of Christianity. Hate him for making humanity! Hate him for making you! Hate him for flinging you into a monstrous life you did not ask for nor deserve! Fill your heart, mind, and soul with hatred, until it's all you know. Until your conscience becomes a firey bomb of hatred for the goodness in your soul. Hate everyone and everything. Hate where you were and are. Hate until you can't anymore. Then learn, read poetry books, philosophy books, history books, science books, write biographies, and autobiographies. Become a sponge for knowledge. Study the philosophies of others and condense the parts you like as your own. Make your own rules. Live by your own laws. For now, truly, you should be at peace with your own true self. Live your life in a bold, new ways. For you, dear friend, are a superhuman.

4-14-97 On Tuesday of last week, I made my first kill. The date was April 12, 1997 about 9:30 p.m. The victim was a loved one. My dear dog Sparkle. Me and an accomplice had been beating the bush for a while and last Tuesday I took a day off from

---

Luke Woodham - a high school shooter in October 1997 at Pearl High School in Pearl, Mississippi. Woodham killed two students and injured seven others at his school but, just prior to that on the same morning, he stabbed and bludgeoned his mother to death in her bed. He has a history of animal abuse in which he tortured and set fire to his own dog "Sparkle". He told the police *"I made my first kill, I sprayed lighter fluid down her throat then her neck caught fire inside and out. It was true beauty."* In June 1998, he was found guilty for three murders and seven counts of aggravated assault. He was given three life sentences and an additional 20 years for each assault charge.

Marie

I don't know how you put up with me all these years. I am not worthy of you, you are the perfect wife you deserve so much better. We had so many good memories together as well as the ~~tragedy~~ tragedy with Elise. It changed my life forever I haven't been the same since it affected me in a way I never felt possible. I am filled with so much hate, hate toward myself hate towards God and unimaginable emptiness it seems like everytime we do something fun I think about how Elise wasn't here to share it with us and I go right back to anger.

Charles Carl Roberts IV - an milk truck driver who murdered five Amish girls before killing himself in an Amish school in the hamlet of Nickel Mines, in Bart Township, Lancaster County, Pennsylvania on October 2, 2006. His father had retired from the police force.

hope we can work together _____ AND, not judge or criticize too harshly @ You know....? @(Smile)
And that fella called "Happy Face Killer"? He is trying to get out of extradition to Colorado, by admitting to a 3rd or 4th murder in Oregon. Crazy huh? The D.A. in that case, already convicted the spouse (man) in killing his wife. So its getting bizarre here. Did you ever write the guy? He's quite the talker I hear.
Hey? Any possibility of me getting any orders from you or any shops? You can trust me to fulfill anything ordered with an invoice _____ Okay?

Friends,

Randall

Randy Woodfield - a serial killer dubbed "The I-5 Killer" or "The I-5 Bandit" for the I-5 Highway running from Washington to California which is where he committed multiple rapes and murders of 18 people. He was convicted of three murders and is incarcerated at the Oregon State Penitentiary. However authorities feel he is the suspect in at least 60 more sexual assaults from the late 1970's to the early 1980's.

Paul John Knowles - (AKA: Lester Daryl Gates, Daryl Golden) and dubbed the "Casanova Killer". He was a spree killer who claimed to have taken 35. While trying to escape from the patrol car during his arrest and, in the process, shooting the driver through his holster, the other officer shot him point black in which he died instantly.

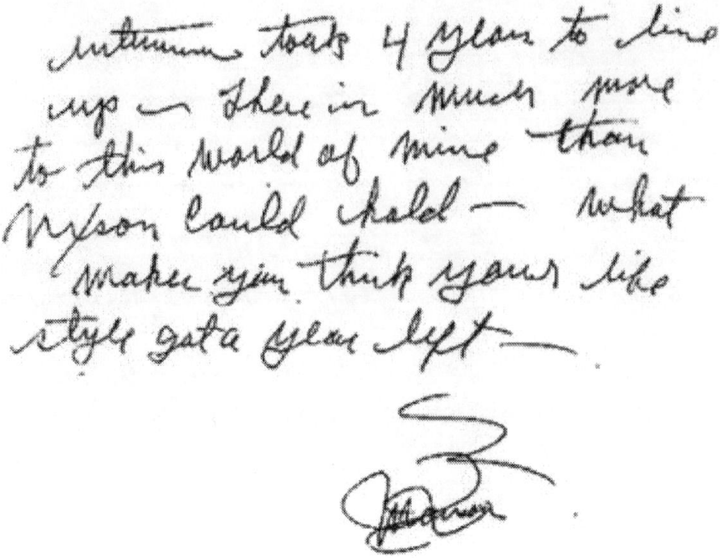

autumn toots 4 years to line
up — There is much more
to this world of mine than
Nixon could hold — what
makes you think your life
style got a year left —

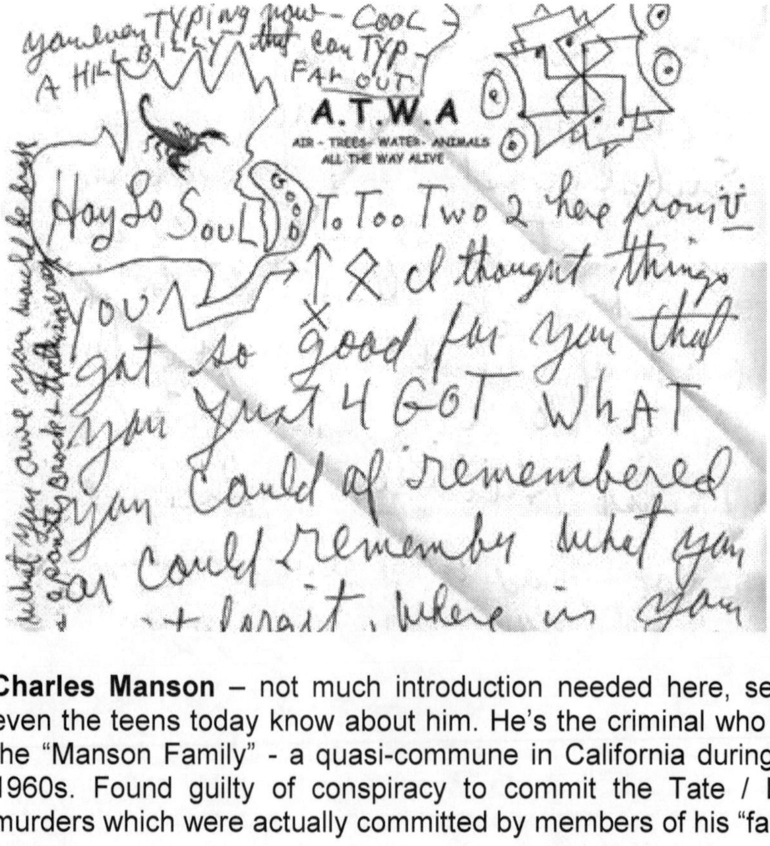

you... TYPing now - CooL
A HILLBILLY that can TYP
FAr OuT

A.T.W.A
AIR - TREES- WATER- ANIMALS
ALL THE WAY ALIVE

Hay Lo SouL To Too Two 2 here from U
& I thought things
got so good for you that
you just 4 GOT WhAT
you could of remembered
or could remember what you
+ forgot. where is you

Charles Manson – not much introduction needed here, seems like even the teens today know about him. He's the criminal who led what the "Manson Family" - a quasi-commune in California during the late 1960s. Found guilty of conspiracy to commit the Tate / LaBianca murders which were actually committed by members of his "family".

Richard Cottingham

Richard Cottingham - a respected family man and father of three who worked as a computer operator. A search of his home turned up a bizarre "trophy room" where he had personal items of several murdered prostitutes, handcuffs, leather gags, two "slave" collars, switchblade knife, a pistol, and several pill bottles. He was a habitual patron of gay bars and homosexual "spas" in New York. He was found guilty on multiple murder counts, and was linked to the brutal abduction and rape of three surviving victims. He was then convicted on 15 felony counts related to another murder giving him a sentence of 173 to 197 years. The following year he was convicted of another murder which was given 20 years to life as his sentence. A couple years later he was again convicted for three murders giving him an additional 75 years to life making his total sentence hundreds of years in length.

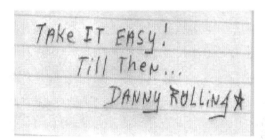

Danny Harold Rolling - a serial killer and son of a police officer who confessed to the murder and mutilation of five students in Gainesville, Florida in August 1990. He was then dubbed "The Gainesville Ripper" and further confessed to raping several of his victims, and committing a triple homicide in Shreveport. He also attempted to kill his abusive father but did not succeed. In total, he admitted to killing eight people. He was found guilty for five first degree murders and was sentenced to death. He was executed on October 25, 2006

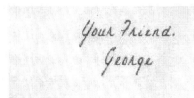

George Putt – serial killer dubbed "Georgie-Boy" and who, by age 18, had been arrested for several counts of violence against women. Psychology tests revealed a "morbid preoccupation with blood and gore" as he continued with his career as a violent criminal. He married in 1967 and brutally forced sexual intercourse with her an average of 8 times per day. He then tried to rape his mother-in-law three times. Shortly afterward he committed his first killing. First he brutally murdered a couple then tied the woman to the bed, raped and mutilated her vagina and anus with a pair of surgical scissors. Just over a week later he beat an 80-year-old widow to death and mutilated her genitalia with a butcher knife. Four days later another woman was bound and brutally stabbed fourteen times. His fifth victim screamed when he entered her home and neighbors called the police. After a chase he was caught trying to escape and smeared in blood. He was found guilty of all his crimes and given the death penalty. When the Supreme Court ended the death penalty he was given a 497-year sentence and, when the judge read his sentence, he laughed.

a few lines to me and spend a little money on me (the material and stamp). Usually, though, it's a letter from someone who wants something from me. My civil attorney wants more information that he can use to make more money on. He, not let me know that my mother and another one trying to contact someone back east that wants to buy memorabilia of mine because I'm supposed to be this infamous serial killer. They are promoting my guilt! One of my brothers wants to sell my car to the highest bidder, touting it as the infamous vehicle of the killer. Again, promoting my guilt! The investigative team that worked on my defense has suddenly turned on me, not wanting anything further to do with me. I've heard that they need something that...

William Suff - a government stock clerk from Riverside County, California, who frequently impersonated police officers, wrote books on violent dogs, drove fancy cars, and volunteered in the community. Dubbed the "Riverside Prostitute Killer" and "Lake Elsinore Killer", people in his neighborhood stated he was "a friendly nerd who was always doing things to help people". He had a prison record in Texas for the 1970's beating his 2-month-old daughter. He was sentenced to 70 years in prison but was paroled after 10 years. He then raped, stabbed, strangled, and randomly mutilated at least 12 prostitutes in Riverside County. All this time, working in his stock clerk job, he frequently delivered supplies to the task force investigating this killing spree. It is said that, in one of his entries in the "Riverside County

Employee Chili Cookoff" he used the breast of one of his victims; ironically that year he won. During a routine traffic stop he was arrested in 1992. After 54 days of testimony and four days of deliberations, the jury found Suff guilty of first-degree murder on 12 counts and one count of attempted murder. He was given the death sentence and most recently was said to be residing on Death Row in San Quentin Prison. While awaiting execution he continues to state he is completely innocent and that the police set him up.

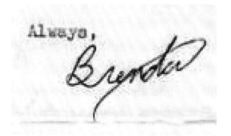

Always,

Brenda

Brenda Spencer - carried out a shooting spree in San Diego, California in January 1979. She opened fire from her house which was located across from Cleveland Elementary School and killed two people while injured nine others. She lived across the street and was well known for stating, "I don't like Mondays". She had an extensive history of abusing cats and dogs most often by setting their tails on fire.

This section will show many handwriting samples from non-famous individuals located throughout the world who have a history and / or arrest records for the abuse of children, animals, and the elderly.

Even if the writer is not "famous", handwriting does not lie. Therefore, the more of the danger indicators you may see in the writing of someone you know… *beware!* While it can take many years for the behaviors to reveal them, the tendencies are there and can become active at any time.

ASK YOURSELF…

"When this person erupts do _I_ want to be around him ?"

If you answered <u>yes</u>... I don't know if that is stupidity or bravery but I will give you my sympathy now while you are still alive to hear it.

If you answered <u>no</u>... that is definitely the intelligent decision that may have saved your life.

Abuse knows no discrimination...

The writers in this next section could be <u>your</u> neighbor, boss, in-law, sibling, child, best friend, teacher, daycare provider, etc.

Here are the directions for cleaning mike's dentures: clean 2x per day. don't use toothpaste bekuz it scratches the pink plastic. and takes off the gloss of the "teeth". Hold one side at a time and work over a sink bekuz they get slippery.

23 year old female from England: although no criminal record, she admits to her extensive history of beating her dogs "when they get in my way". She also stated she has been the aggressor with relationships and has an anger issue. By the way, each dog was adopted from an animal rescue.

happy birthday honey! love Julie

42 year old male from USA: extensive criminal history for the physical assault of his elderly parents and developmentally delayed sister. Ironically people were shocked when he was arrested for the first time because they stated, "he got along great with everyone and seemed so nice". So did Ted Bundy and those that said that he was nice later most certainly have regret about doing so.

we had a great time in Maryland and Rhode Island. The trip was too short. The other states were nice too but they were our favorites by far.

28 year old female from Australia: history of being diagnosed Bipolar and mutilating dogs and cats "only when frustrated".

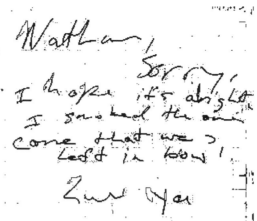

33 year old male from USA: sentenced to 14 years for multiple aggravated assaults and rape. Extensive history of domestic violence with now-ex wife whom he stalked for 2 years before raping her at gunpoint.

I had a dream that I was eating supper with my family and I was very happy. Now if I can apologize and get my family to talk to me sometime. I get so lonely without them.

17 year old female from Germany: in front of her mother she strangled her mother's cat and punched her 3 month old baby sister because her mother did not grant permission for her to attend a slumber party.

have a drink on me and my friends will be happy to make you food too!

Maggie

47 year old female from USA: history of stalked her boyfriend and, in one instance, she got into the back of his van and waited until he got in. As soon as he did, she stabbed him in the arm twice with a scissors

My wife's name is Mindy and we argue all the time. She makes me very angryy !!!!!

63 year old male from Australia: incarcerated for the aggravated sexual assault of a child. He held the child at knife point. He had been investigated for inappropriate sexual relations with several of his pets.

Michele I am really sorry for pissing you off but I think you over-reacted and for that "go fuck yourself" and when you are at it "not in hell" too !

32 year old female from Canada: she was arrested for filming pornographic movies with her children and selling them online and to a production company in the southeast USA. Several of these movies involved their family pets in inappropriate positions and doing inappropriate sexual things with her children. When she was questioned by police she repeatedly lied about it to obscure the investigation.

...ove, and over and over I feel I...
...have too many people wanting too much...
...from me and I'm sick of it already.

25 year old female from Australia: history of being diagnosed Bipolar and mutilating dogs and cats "only when frustrated".

- life puts in our way
overcome it. It's like the
sint kill you makes you
And I firmly believe th

37 year old male from USA: at the time of this writing, he was incarcerated for several "aggravated domestic violence and terroristic threats". He has a history of extensive drug abuse and beating the household pets to emotionally traumatize his children and wife to gain compliance.

Magical Moment is my favorite song on CD. I
like the piano sound with the rain most.

62 year old female from Belgium: according to her children she has been "argumentative and mean all her life and would never listen to the opinions of others – even if facts were included". They included, "and when she got mad at her dog, she would punch "Lulu" in the face".

I used to do a lot of sports but now I hate to exercise at all.

38 year old male from USA: he has five "flags" in the humane society for adopting dogs and then turning them in severely diseased, neglected, and / or physically and drastically wounded.

we just announced that we will be moving to Tennessee in March and then we will consider moving into a house when we know where.

37 year old female from USA: she was charged with multiple felony counts of the physical abuse and neglect of her elderly parents. The parents are both deceased which happened to be within 6 months of her being charged..

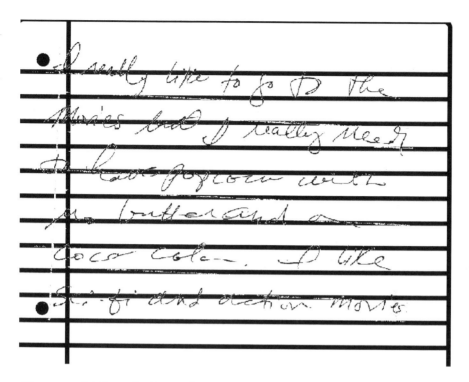

I really like to go to the
movies but I really need
to eat popcorn with
a butter and a
coca cola. I like
sci-fi and action movies

61 year old female from Canada: while living in the USA she served time in prison for sexual assault of a minor, attempted murder of an elderly couple for financial gain, and admitted a childhood fixation on death and participated in satanic rituals on Halloween where she actively participated in the vicious sacrificing of multiple animals. She even stated, "I knew some were my friends or neighbors pets but they should have kept them inside".

that's not funny at all
because I could have gotten
hurt don't do that again.

47 year old male from USA: lifetime of "bar fights, arguments, spousal abuse, and anything violent he can get into". He would get his dogs drunk on beer and videotape it stating it was his 'favorite hobby'. He then beat his Rottweiler repeatedly with a board when he was bad that, one day, the Rottweiler turned on him attacking him viciously. A neighbor heard the scuffle and shot the dog.

Diamonds - swish around in a solution of 1 tblsp. of amonia and 1C. hot water. Then dip in rubbing alcohol and pat dry with tissue paper. Or you can use a commercial jewel cleaner and follow instructions on the bottle.

---

73 year old female from USA: she was a hoarder of cats and small dots. She stated she was "helping the homeless animals" but the neighbors complained to police and rescue groups wanted to find them new homes. Initially cooperative, before anyone could rescue them from her, she killed them all by crushing their skulls with the claw side of the hammer. She then piled their bodies in the empty pool of her house and set them on fire. Neighbors called the police and reported hearing "horrifying animal cries" but authorities were too late. The authorities believe some animals were still alive when the fire started to burn their bodies.

Had to get a new hard drive for my Computer today.

---

39 year old male from Japan: he was known for beating his wife and forcing sexual intercourse upon her at knifepoint while the kids watched saying "Your mom is a whore".

Mary are you and Richard sure of the trip to Michigan in March - its probably still going to be cold and snowing there!

---

56 year old male from USA: he was known in his circle of friends and relatives for 'threatening to kill people that are stupid and worthless because they waste this countries resources including air'. One day he grabbed his 14 year old son, held the side of his head to a hot burner and, while scalding him, yelled stating "Maybe this will make you use your brain". When his wife called police he shot her.

How to be happy: wake up with a smile and it can make you have good and happy dreams too. If you dream happy then your life is okay!

34 year old female from Mexico: while living in the USA she was accused of inappropriate sexual acts with her four year old son but charges were dropped due to no complaining witness and no evidence. She was however prosecuted for neglect and her parental rights were severed. That's when she moved to Mexico.

Last night we went singing at Theresa's Good Time and sang and danced with the band all nite.

59 year old female from USA: she was known as the "meanest biker chick in the county – nobody messed with her" said her brother. He continued, "She would do crazy things like pull people out of their car and threaten with a knife if they drove too slow or cut her off".

Banana Nut Muffins. are my favorite and taste really good with orange juice in the morning.

29 year old female from France: she was known as the "only female in the family with a man's strong personality". She loved a good debate and, when it turned into an argument, she somehow made sure she would have the very last word.

I really need to update my resume so maybe I can find a job again. My family always calls me a loser.

29 year old male from Europe: he admitted to having a bizarre sexual appetite and was hoping to find work in an all-woman company so there was "no competition". He stated he practiced bestiality "only when I'm not in a relationship but I am hoping my next woman will be into that as well".

Julia and Gary will probably have the wedding at their house in the very pretty part of our country known as the Hamptons!

46 year old female from USA: she was known as the 'stuck up' one and, of all her friends she would be *the* one to never say, or do anything immoral, illegal, or unethical. She was convicted of having sadistic sexual relations with a minor. Her children's testimonies led to her conviction of child abuse.

my daughter is my only challenge in life but even though she is, I still love her on most days!

24 year old female from USA: she was the aggressor in the domestic violence charges on her record as well as the severe physical abuse of her 9 year old daughter.

Thanks for Nothing at all and do me a favor and do not come over here ever again because you do not make any sense to me with what you do!

44 year old male from Germany: he was known to lose his temper easily and then "fight it off with whomever was around". He was also known to beat his dog when he was a puppy.

Some of of my fave singers are are Patty loveless and Carrie Underwood

33 year old female from USA: she was known as "heartless" whenever she heard tales of woe. She would, in fact, ask the victims what they did to deserve it. One of her former best friends was upset due to the abuse of her husband. This writer said, "If you whined to him like you are with me I'd beat your ass too so you probably deserved it". She then told her that it would not happen if she wasn't such a baby and to 'toughen up' and deal with it.

We are excited to move to Florida and get new jobs. He works in Accounting and I Usually work in Property Management.

26 year old female from USA: she was known to be violent in random, sporadic times and who suffered from anxiety in new situations. She has a diagnosis of Bipolar but she disagrees and refuses medication. She has a history of assault and says, "if people didn't make me so mad I wouldn't have to beat their ass".

Happy Birthday Morgan – you are now 13 and I am so proud of you.
Love Mom and Mindy

52 year old female from England: she was known to be argumentative and a "military style mom". Her daughter stated she was mean most of the time but, when she decided to be a good mom, she was excellent so it was easy to forgive her for the mixed messages.

I really like my job because it gives me free travel and I get to meet a lot of new people.

32 year old female from USA: she was caught performing oral sex on her 10 year old boy and has a history of multiple underage relations but was never convicted of any for various reasons including lack of evidence. At one time she stated, "I should be an elementary teacher".

Many times I feel like everyone hates me but I can't help it. I am Me and they are them.

18 year old female from USA: she has an excessive drug abuse problem and states it is because "everyone hates me". She admits she is moody and one minute can be "super nice and then super bitch and beat everyone around me". She has history of assaulting animals with various objects inserted into their rectums. She also states she "gives my male dogs hand-jobs when I'm frustrated but they love it".

I have a hard time sleeping at nite.
My husband thinks its because my
brain never shuts off.

26 year old female from USA: she is a writer who specializes in violence and brutality for themes. She says she has a "mind of my own and do what I want in my own life and the lives of my characters".

Dally and me are going to the Mall
of America to go shopping for Christmas.
Maybe Robert and Mike will join us!

37 year old female from USA: she is referred to as the 'tough one' in her circle of friends having survived in abusive relationships, overcome alcohol addiction, sexual assaults as a child, and more. What they don't know is that she abuses her elderly mother who has an advanced stage of Alzheimer's.

I have to have coke to drink and when I
eat I have to have Ketchup on almost
everything. My family calls me the
"Ketchup freak".

32 year old male from Canada: he is a self-proclaimed loner and feels forced to spend time with his family. A closet alcoholic he works or plays games on computers and, when frustrated, self-mutilates. He states he cannot even feel the razor blade on his abdomen anymore because he's insensitive to the pain "after all these years".

THE MOVIE EVITA MAKES ALMOST
EVERYONE I KNOW CRY. I DONT
UNDERSTAND WHY.

58 year old male from USA: he has been told he has a "split personality" because he is "never the same – I'm so different all the time I don't even know a thing about myself". His criminal record includes four counts of aggravated assault, two counts of attempted murder, and rape.

My dog barks at everything even when I don't see anything to bark at if I were a dog.

26 year old female from USA: she and her husband openly practice bestiality and belong to a large private club of the same act. She stated the "animals seem to enjoy it and so do we". She went on to say, "we aren't hurting them we are loving them and they are loving us back".

Dinn*

You know that was no knife but a plastic spoon I dont wont to hurt you but I dont wont you to B afraid diane I paid the rent. you got to let me talk to you I will get your money

24 year old male from USA: he has extensive history of being the aggressor in domestic violence incidents. On one occasion he beat his wife so badly she was nearly in a coma. On another occasion he beat his wife's cat to death in front of her while she was chained to the chair. On another occasion he strangled his dog because he barked too much.

the first fantasy I told you about. I think you've got the mind for both of them, actually, but I'm not willing to lose our friendship over this. I told you I was a pervert though — and now you see what I meant. If there is any way that you would be cool with my fantasies — maybe you could send me a little tease. You can feel free to make something up — but I'll tell you a little something of what I like. Have you ever seen According To Jim? The girls on there are very cute. OK — well I think that's enough for now. For all I know you could write me back and tell me to get lost. I'm really hoping that you'll understand that's it's only thoughts — not reality — and I'm hoping that you've seen enough of the real

45 year old male from USA: he is serving time for sexual abuse of a minor. He has extensive fantasies of incest that he admits to. He asks the women who have the hobby of "writing inmates" to send pictures of their young girls when they are naked or at slumber parties and then professes his love for each of the women. He admits he is *"sick but I don't feel it is wrong"*.

Survival Guide

Use this checklist to 'stack' traits that you find. In other words, the more danger signs you find, the more danger you may be in. **Stay away and protect yourself**. Don't forget to utilize 9-1-1 or other legal avenues for assistance.

Anti-Social Personality Disorder (ASPD) is a personality disorder that involves pervasive disregard for the rights and boundaries of others. This includes behaviors that are impulsive, irresponsible and aggressive. Those with ASPD, whether clinically diagnosed or not, tend to be involved in crime, domestic violence, drug and / or alcohol abuse, rape and murder. They tend to break every moral and social rule without ever feeling remorseful. ASPD is usually preceded by serious and persistent conduct problems starting in early childhood so this makes it easier to identify those that are at-risk.

Here is an **ANTI-SOCIAL CHECKLIST** to help decipher if someone may have ASPD:

_____ **Superficial Charm** – why everyone thinks he is "such a nice guy". They depend on you to think that.

_____ **Manipulative and Cunning** – he ignores the rights and boundaries of others. He appears charming, but is covertly hostile and domineering. Without hesitation he easily uses his victim and may dominate and humiliate them.

_____ **Grandiose**– he feels entitled to certain things as "his right" (usually accompanied by narcissism).

_____ **Pathological Lying** – he lies easily and calmly; it is near impossible for him to be truthful. He easily creates, and believes own powers, abilities and lies – even beats polygraphs

_____ **Lack of Remorse, Shame or Guilt** – he has a deep-seeded but repressed rage which drives him. He looks at the world as an opportunity as long as he can eliminate opposition in any way possible. Don't worry – he will justify the means.

_____ **Shallow Emotions** – he fakes any show of warmth, happiness, love, and compassion but always has an ulterior motive. He become very angry about trivial things and is unaffected by things that upset the general public. His thoughts and emotions are not sincere so don't believe any promises he makes to you as they will not be sincere either.

____ **Incapacity for Love** – he is unable to form and maintain healthy relationships because he is incapable of feeling and experiencing true love.

____ **Need for Stimulation** – he is a rule-breaker who lives on the edge. Typical behaviors include verbal insults and physical outbursts. Sex and gambling addictions are very common.

____ **Callousness / Lack of Empathy** – because he is incapable of true feelings of any kind, he is not able to empathize with the pain of his victim. He only has contempt for others' in distress and will quickly take advantage of them.

____ **Poor Behavior and Impulse Control** – he will show acts of rage and abuse, then small expressions of love and approval (the "honeymoon" stage), and then back to rage and abuse again. This causes co-dependency between the abuser and his victim and the victim feels hopeless and powerless. He will then believe he is all-powerful, all-knowing, entitled to everything he wants, with no sense of personal boundaries, and no concern for how he hurts others.

____ **Early Behavioral Problems and / or Juvenile Delinquency** – he likely has a history of behavioral issues and problems in school but somehow manages to "get by". He probably has problems making and maintaining friends and strong likelihood to be cruelty to people or animals, and other criminal acts.

____ **Irresponsibility / Unreliability** – he is not concerned about wrecking the lives of other people and has no concern for any problems he causes others because he will blame someone else for his acts no matter the evidence against him.

____ **Promiscuous Sexual Behavior and Infidelity** – acting promiscuous and having random sexual "flings"; he could easily commit child sexual abuse, rape and other sexual urges without concern for the victims or consequences.

___ **Parasitic Lifestyle** - he tends to change residences a lot, mooching off of others, and may even mention all kinds of "plans for the future" yet has poor work ethic and usually no intention of follow through. However he will be sure to continue exploiting others to reach his goals effectively.

___ **Criminal Entrepreneurial Skills** – he changes his image as needed to avoid prosecution and, along with his image, his life history changes to match.

ASPD Personality Indicators:

1. Irritated by them who seek to understand them
2. Does not feel anything is wrong with them
3. Authoritarian attitude
4. Secretive lifestyle
5. Paranoid behaviors or thoughts
6. Common problems with the law and know their tyrannical behavior will be tolerated, condoned, or admired in prison
7. Appear "normal" – that's part of their manipulation
8. Goal of "owning" and "controlling" their victims
9. Exercises power and control in a cruel and unreasonable way within every aspect of their victim's life
10. Has an emotional need to justify their crimes and therefore needs their victim's respect, gratitude and love
11. Their goal is always to have a willing victim
12. Not capable of feeling attachment for another human
13. Not capable of feeling guilt or remorse
14. Extremely narcissistic and grandiose
15. Readily say that they would like, or will, rule the world

(The above list is based on the psychopathy checklist of R. Hare.)

SYNOPSIS

These have a consistent lack of regard for the rights and feelings of others – whether human or animal. They have a conduct disorder before age 15 and have a history of illegal activities whether or not they have been caught and / or convicted. They are slippery and difficult to catch because they lie, cheat, steal, are irresponsible, cannot maintain relationships unless they "gain" something from it and have no remorse. It is believed that those from an abusive or neglected upbringing are more prone to this disorder.

DANGERS: prone to be imprisoned for their behaviors. They are very aggressive, get into fights frequently, have extremely high amounts of interpersonal problems and are completely untrustworthy and unpredictable. They have great superficial charm – they are the "con-men" who won't do anything for anyone other than himself unless there is something for him to gain. There are no treatments for ASPD because it would require honesty and openness in order to build rapport with the therapist. They are incapable of this and nearly immediately sabotage their treatment. Today's traditional methods of psychotherapy (psychoanalysis, group and one-on-one therapy) and psychological medications have failed. Therapy is more likely to work when an individual admits there's a problem and wants to change. The common problem with psychopaths is they see nothing wrong with their behaviors.

Dr. Hare's Psychopathy Survival Guide

People must know what they're dealing with. Psychopaths are found in every strata of society and can manipulate and con anyone, including mental health experts. The best protection is to understand the nature of these predatory beasts. One should try not to be influenced by the façade that's created by a psychopath.

Psychopaths have a repertoire of non-verbal language including a penetrating stare and dramatic body movements. Ignore these or look away; listen carefully to the words. Don't be blind; psychopaths hide their dark side and wear a mask of flattery, false concern, pathological lies and deceit.

If the person is too good to be true, be hyper-vigilant. Be guarded in risky or too-relaxed situations including singles bars, churches, and other groups. People must know themselves. Psychopaths are uncannily skilled at finding and exploiting the weaknesses of others. Guard against people who aim for weak spots. Lonely well-to-do people are their favorite targets so be aware who the victim is. Psychopaths play the role of the victim by using pity parties and other methods while they exploit others.

There are several types:

1. **The charming type** - have personal charm through which they manage to contact their victims and gain trust.
2. **The ambitious type** - have strong ambitions otherwise they would not risk their lives and freedom.
3. **The security man** - have the ability to keep their secret to themselves, often stalk their victim, and plan the murder or the assault without sharing it with others.
4. **The obsessive** - all the serial killers obsessively repeat their horrible crimes.
5. **The criminal** - have a captivating charm and ability to pretend and conceal their true intentions. They can lie without a blink, a hesitation, and completely lack conscience.
6. **The destructive type** - destructive instincts cause them to murder and, by killing, they destroy their victims and in most cases themselves as well.

We can conclude that they all share characteristics which are extremely twisted.

THE MALIGNANT PERSONALITY

These people are mentally ill and **extremely dangerous**! The following precautions will help to protect you from the destructive acts of which they are capable. First, to recognize them, keep the following guidelines in mind:

(1) They are **habitual liars**. They seem incapable of either knowing or telling the truth about anything.
(2) They are **egotistical** to the point of **narcissism**. They really believe they are set apart from the rest of humanity by some special grace.
(3) They **scapegoat**; they are incapable of either having the insight or willingness to accept responsibility for anything they do. Whatever the problem, it is always someone else's fault.
(4) They are **remorselessly vindictive** when thwarted or exposed.
(5) Genuine religious, moral, or other values play **no part** in their lives. They have no empathy for others and are capable of violence. Under older psychological terminology, they fall into the category of psychopath or sociopath, but unlike the typical psychopath, their behavior is masked by a **superficial social facade.**

If you have come into conflict with such a person or persons, do the following immediately!

(1) **Notify** your friends and relatives of what has happened.

Do not be vague. Name names, and specify dates and circumstances. Identify witnesses if possible and provide supporting documentation if any is available.

(2) **Inform** the police. The police will do nothing with this information except to keep it on file, since they are powerless to act until a crime has been committed. Unfortunately, that often is usually too late for the victim. Nevertheless, place the information in their hands.

Obviously, if you are assaulted or threatened before witnesses, you can get a restraining order, but those are palliative at best.

(3) Local law enforcement agencies are usually under pressure if wealthy or politically powerful individuals are involved, so **include** state and federal agencies as well and tell the locals that you have. The FBI is an important agency to contact, because although the FBI does not have jurisdiction over murder or assault, if informed, they do have an active interest in any other law enforcement agencies that do not follow through with an honest investigation and prosecution should a murder occur. Civil rights are involved at that point. No local crooked lawyer, judge, or corrupt police official wants to be within a country mile if that comes to light! It is in such cases that wealthy psychopaths discover just how firm the "friends" they count on to cover up for them really are! Even some of the drug cartel biggies will scuttle for cover if someone picks up the brick their thugs hide under. **Exposure** is bad for business.

(4) Make sure that **several** of your friends have the information in the event something happens to you. That way, an appropriate investigation will follow if you are harmed. Don't tell other people who has the information, because then something bad could happen to them as well. Instruct friends to take such an incident to the newspapers and other media.

The Anti-Social Script

Eight out of 10 murders and violent abusers write with a very high level of 'ASPD" style. **Therefore let's talk about their handwriting**…

Freud's "Id" represents the **lower portion of handwriting** which is our physical, sexual appetites that, as the writing reveals, can become too demanding and take control forcing the brutality and aggression. The "Super-ego" is the **upper part of our writing** and controls are urges, our moral level of right vs. wrong and our conscious. When the "Superego" is working properly it should be able to control the "Id" to **prevent the violent follow-through**. Therefore the remorse, empathy, logic and judgment are missing.

While I recommend you utilize the graphic and corresponding sections of this book, sometimes you don't have the time to do so. Therefore below is the most prominent strokes to be aware of. Below is a **snapshot of their handwriting**. The more of these graphic signs you have, the more likely **you are in danger !**

- Tense or overly-controlled handwriting
- Extremely heavy pressure
- Narrow or skinny letters and loops
- Extremely wide spaces between words or excessively close
- Retraced or coiled strokes
- Too tall upper or lower loops
- Extreme left or right slant
- Inconsistent pressure
- A lot of sharp strokes
- Inappropriate x-shapes, illegible letters, or weapons
- Thick letter endings
- Weird twists in letters
- Broken or stencil-like letters
- "Felon's Claws" or "stingers"

With all the technology available to us today there is no reason not to use it… it may save your life!

Here's a great example:

As of September 3, 2010 Thomas Kane, Arizona Inmate # 60051 has a singles ad online at http://www.cyberspace-inmates.com/kanet.htm

His <u>handwriting sample</u> is on the next page and is **very disturbing !**

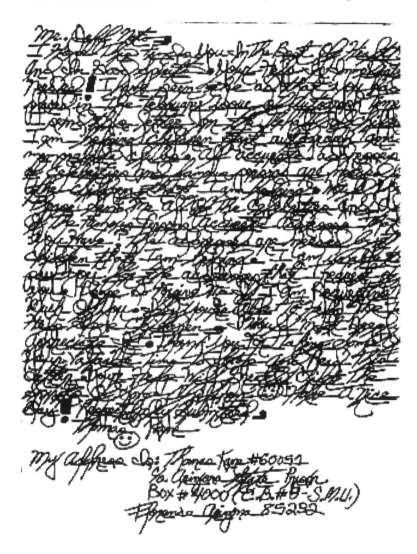

As of September 2010 his public criminal record can be found online at the following website...

http://www.azcorrections.gov/inmate_datasearch/results.aspx?In mateNumber=060051&LastName=KANE&FNMI=T&SearchType =SearchInet

Let's look at his **criminal record** on the site above.

Inmate 060051
T KANE

Last Name	First Name	Middle Initial	Birth Date
KANE	THOMAS	P	12/27/1961
Gender	**Height (inches)**	**Weight**	**Hair Color**
MALE	64	135	BLACK
Eye Color	**Ethnic Origin**	**Custody Class**	**Inmate / Detainee**
BROWN	CAUCASIAN	5/5	INMATE
Sentence (yyymmdd)	**Admission**	**Prison Release Date**	**Max End Date**
020/00/00	10/27/1986		04/26/2026

Cur. Absconded	Hist. Absconded	Release Type	Most Recent Loc.	Unit
--	--	RECEIVED AT	ASPC Eyman	

Community Supervision/ Parole		Last Movement	Commitment Status	Status
N		09/28/2009	COMPLETE AND VERIFIED	ACTIVE

Articles on Anti-Social Personality Disorder

Early Signs of Psychopathy (ASPD)

New Study of Toddlers Identifies Antecedents of Antisocial Behavior

Aug 19, 2007 by Tami Port

Study published in August 2007 issue of The Journal of Abnormal Psychology indicates that some traits correlating to adult psychopathy b may be present as early as age 3.

A twenty-five year study, published this month in *The Journal of Abnormal Psychology*, demonstrates that, as early as the age of three, there are temperamental and physiological difference between those who show psychopathic tendencies as adults and those who don't.

What Is a Psychopath?

Psychopathy, also known as Anti-social Personality (APD or ASPD), is a psychological personality disorder. Not only do psychopaths lack emotions of conscience and empathy, but research has shown that these individuals consistently display certain aspects of temperament including a lack of fear, lack of inhibition and stimulus seeking behavior. Psychopathic adults have also demonstrated physiological idiosyncrasies, such as a reduced physical response to negative stimuli, and indifference to the threat of pain and punishment (Hare 1999).

Traits Predictive of Psychopathy

The *Journal of Abnormal Psychology* published the first long-term study to examine very young children for traits predictive of adult psychopathy. The team of researchers hypothesized that psychopathic adults would, as young children, be expected to show less fear and inhibition and more stimulus seeking/sociable behavior than adults who did not develop psychopathy. The researchers also predicted that, since adult psychopaths show reduced sensitivity to negative stimuli, this response would also be apparent at an early age.

Psychopathy Assessment of Children

Between 1972 and 1973, 1,795 three-year-olds, from the island of Mauritius, were enrolled in the study, and each observed and rated on several variables related to inhibited/disinhibited temperament, stimulation seeking/sociability and fearfulness/reactivity. Physiological reaction to stimuli was also assessed by monitoring skin conductivity (SC) in response to both neutral and aversive noise.

Skin conductivity startle response is a well studied physiological reaction caused by sympathetic nervous system activation. This response corresponds to measures of emotion, arousal, and attention. In this study, skin conductivity was painlessly measured, with leads on the first and second fingers of the left hand.

Psychopathy Assessment of Adults

Twenty-five years later, the researchers were able to complete follow-up assessments on 335 of the adults who had been originally evaluated as children. The subjects were tested for psychopathic traits using the Self-Report Psychopathy Scale (SRP-II), a 60 item modified version of Dr. Robert Hare's Psychopathy Checklist Revised (PCL-R).

Born to Be Psychopaths?

The investigators found that adults with higher psychopathy scores had marked differences as 3 year olds, being significantly less fearful/inhibited and more stimulus seeking/sociable than those adults who had lower psychopathy scores. With respect to physiologic response, the group with higher SRP-II scores had significantly reduced sensitivity to negative auditory stimuli as toddlers.

Fear and Morality

Kochanska (1993) has suggested that the normal fearfulness most children experience contributes to development of moral emotions like guilt, empathy and shame. Children who are more fearful are prone to remorse after doing wrong and are more concerned about the consequences of their behavior; a concern that typically deters them from future wrongdoings. The results of this study suggest that children with a low level of fearfulness may be more likely to develop antisocial personality as adults.

Sociability and Psychopathy

Sociability and seeking stimulation are traits often associated with the glibness, charm and manipulation shown by adult psychopaths, and this study did indicate that individuals testing psychopathic as adults had higher stimulus/seeking and sociability scores as three year olds.

Negative Stimuli and Psychopathic Traits

Lastly, the physiological reaction of longer skin conductivity recovery time, in response to negative stimuli, has been linked to impairment in a person's inclination to avoid harm or physical danger. This reduced sensitivity to negative stimuli is characteristic of adult psychopaths, and, in this study, was significantly more pronounced in the 3 year olds who developed psychopathic traits as adults.

Additional Research on Inheritance of Psychopathy

A study of twins, published in June 2005 issue of *the Journal of Child Psychology and Psychiatry*, revealed that anti-social behavior is strongly inherited in children with psychopathic tendencies such as callousness and reduced emotional capacity.

Understanding Psychopathy

Although this research is preliminary, it may help to increase our understanding of psychopathy and eventually provide information on ways to prevent antisocial criminal behavior. Other resources on psychopathy and personality disorders in general include: Psychology Prof Online, The Mayo Clinic: Mental Health Center and the following articles:

Hare, R.D. (1999) *Without Conscience: The Disturbing World of Psychopaths Among Us.* Guiford Press.

Hare, R. D. (1985) Comparison of procedures for the assessment of psychopathy. *Journal of Consulting and Clinical Psychology.* 53, 7.

Portrait of a Sociopath

From Craig, M., Catani, M., Deeley, Q., Latham, R., Daly, E., Kanaan, R., Picchioni, M., McGuire, P., Fahy, T., & Murphy, D. (2009). Altered connections on the road to psychopathy Molecular Psychiatry, 14 (10), 946-953 DOI: 10.1038/mp.2009.40

The manipulative con-man. The guy who lies to your face, even when he doesn't have to. The child who tortures animals. The cold-blooded killer. Psychopaths are characterized by an absence of empathy and poor impulse control, with a total lack of conscience. About 1% of the total population can be defined as psychopaths, according to a detailed psychological profile checklist. They tend to be egocentric, callous, manipulative, deceptive, superficial, irresponsible and parasitic, even predatory. The majority of psychopaths are not violent and many do very well in jobs where their personality traits are advantageous and their social tendencies tolerated. However, some have a predisposition to calculated, "instrumental" violence; violence that is cold-blooded, planned and goal-directed. Psychopaths are vastly over-represented among criminals; it is estimated they make up about 20% of the inmates of most prisons. They commit over half of all violent crimes and are 3-4 times more likely to re-offend. They are almost entirely refractory to rehabilitation. These are not nice people.

So how did they get that way? Is it an innate biological condition, a result of social experience, or an interaction between these factors? Longitudinal studies have shown that the personality traits associated with psychopathy are highly stable over time. Early warning signs including "callous-unemotional traits" and antisocial behavior can be identified in childhood and are highly predictive of future psychopathy. Large-scale twin studies have shown that these traits are highly heritable – identical twins, who share 100% of their genes, are much more similar to each other in this trait than fraternal twins, who share only 50% of their genes. In one study, over 80% of the variation in the callous-unemotional trait across the population was due to genetic differences. In contrast, the effect of a shared family environment was almost nil. Psychopathy seems to be a lifelong trait, or combination of traits, which are heavily influenced by genes and hardly at all by social upbringing.

The two defining characteristics of psychopaths, blunted emotional response to negative stimuli, coupled with poor impulse control, can both be measured in psychological and neuro-imaging experiments. Several studies have found decreased responsiveness of the amygdala to fearful or other negative stimuli in psychopaths. They do not seem to process heavily loaded emotional words, like "rape", for example, any differently from how they process neutral words, like "table". This lack of response to negative stimuli can be measured in other ways, such as the failure to induce a galvanic skin response (heightened skin conduction due to sweating) when faced with an impending electrical shock. Psychopaths have also been found to under-activate limbic (emotional) regions of the brain during aversive learning, correlating with insensitivity to negative reinforcement. The psychopath really just doesn't care. In this, psychopaths differ from many people who are prone to sudden, impulsive violence, in that those people tend to have a hypersensitive negative emotional response to what would otherwise be relatively innocuous stimuli.

What these two groups have in common is poor impulse control. This faculty relies on the part of the brain called the prefrontal cortex, most particularly the orbit-frontal cortex. It is known that lesions to this part of the brain impair planning, prediction of consequences, and inhibition of socially unacceptable behavior – the cognitive mechanisms of "free won't", rather than free will. This brain region is also normally activated by aversive learning, and this activation is also reduced in psychopaths. In addition, both the prefrontal cortex and the amygdala show substantial average reductions in size in psychopaths, suggesting a structural difference in their brains.

These findings have now been united by a recent study that directly analyzed connectivity between these two regions. Using diffusion tensor imaging (see post of August 31st 2009), Craig and colleagues found that a measure of the integrity of the axonal tract connecting these two regions, called the uncinate fasciculus, was significantly reduced in psychopaths. Importantly, connectivity of these regions to other parts of the brain was normal. These data thus suggest a specific disruption of the network connecting orbit-frontal cortex and amygdala in psychopaths, the degree of which correlated strongly with the subjects' scores on the psychopathy checklist.

All of these findings are pointing to a picture of psychopathy as an innate, genetically driven difference in connectivity between parts of the brain that normally drive empathy, conscience and impulse control.

Not a fault necessarily, and not something that could be classified as a disease or that is always a disadvantage. At a certain frequency in the population, the traits of psychopathy may be highly advantageous to the individual.

This conclusion has serious ethical and legal implications. Could a psychopath mount a legal defense by saying "my brain made me do it"? Or my "genes made me do it"? Is this any different from saying my rotten childhood made me do it? Psychopaths know right from wrong – they just don't care. That is what society calls "bad", not "mad". But if they are constitutionally incapable of caring, can they really be blamed for it? On the other hand, if violent psychopaths are a continuing danger to society and completely refractory to rehabilitation, what is to be done with them? Perhaps, as has been proposed in the UK, people with the extreme psychopathic personality profile (or maybe in the near future even a specific genetic profile?) should be monitored or segregated even before they commit a crime.

While it is crucial that these debates are informed by good science, these issues have no clear-cut answers. They will be resolved on a pragmatic basis, weighing the behavior that society is willing to tolerate versus the rights of the individual, whatever their brains look like, to define their own moral standards.

The Unburdened Mind

Written by Christopher S. Putnam on 20 January 2008

"I don't think I feel things the same way you do."

The man sits at the table in the well-fitted attire of success—charming, witty, and instantly likeable. He is a confident, animated speaker, but he seems to be struggling with this particular point.

"It's like... at my first job," he continues, "I was stealing maybe a thousand bucks a month from that place. And this kid, he was new, he got wise. And he was going to turn me in, but before he got the chance I went to the manager and pinned the whole thing on him." Now he is grinning widely. "Kid lost his job, the cops got involved, and I don't know what happened to him. And I guess something like that is supposed to make me feel bad, right? It's supposed to hurt, right? But instead, it's like there's nothing." He smiles apologetically and shakes his head. "Nothing."

His name is Frank, and he is a psychopath.

In the public imagination, a "psychopath" is a violent serial killer or an over-the-top movie villain, as one sometimes might suspect Frank to be. He is highly impulsive and has a callous disregard for the well-being of others that can be disquieting. But he is just as likely to be a next-door neighbor, a doctor, or an actor on TV—essentially no different from anyone else who holds these roles, except that Frank lacks the nagging little voice which so profoundly influences most of our lives. Frank has no conscience. And as much as we would like to think that people like him are a rare aberration, safely locked away, the truth is that they are more common than most would ever guess.

"My mother, the most beautiful person in the world. She was strong, she worked hard to take care of four kids. A beautiful person. I started stealing her jewelry when I was in the fifth grade. You know, I never really knew the bitch — we went our separate ways." –Hare, *Without Conscience: The Disturbing World of the Psychopaths Among Us*

The word *psychopathy* dates back in an early form to the 19th century, but as a modern term it's primarily used in reference to the work of Canadian psychologist Robert Hare. Hare's *PCL-R* tool (Psychopathy Checklist – Revised) was developed to test for a wide range of socially deviant behaviors and personality traits, the most important being the absence of any sense of conscience, remorse, or guilt. The result of this combination is a destructive, self-serving, and often dangerous individual sometimes called "the born criminal."

The psychopath's world is a strikingly skewed one in which the normal laws of human emotion and interaction do not apply—yet it serves as reality for a sizable portion of humanity. Spanning all cultures and eras, roughly one man in every 100 is born a clinical psychopath, as well as one woman in every 300. They are so common that every person reading this sentence almost certainly knows one personally; indeed, a significant number of readers are likely psychopaths themselves.

Many potential psychopaths might not even realize they have the condition, nor has there traditionally been any easy way for others to recognize them. The leading scientific test is Hare's PCL-R, but to be valid it must be performed by a qualified professional under controlled conditions. For those who can't be bothered with such expensive frills, we present the PCL-DI: an alternative, PCL-inspired test guaranteed to appear scientific.

The concept of the psychopath is only the latest and most refined in a long string of attempts to account for a certain pattern of conduct. In the 19th century, psychiatric clinicians began to notice patients in their care who fit no known diagnosis, but who nevertheless displayed strange and disturbing behaviors. They were impulsive and self-destructive. They had no regard for the feelings and welfare of others. They lied pathologically, and when caught, they shrugged it off with a smirk and moved on to the next lie. It was a puzzle—because while there was clearly something unusual about these patients, they showed none of the psychotic symptoms or defects in reason thought necessary for mental illness at the time. Indeed, apart from a tendency to follow foolish and irresponsible impulses that sometimes got them into trouble, they were coldly rational—more rational, perhaps, than the average citizen. Their condition therefore came to be referred to as *manie sans délire* ("insanity without delirium"), a term which later evolved into *moral insanity* once the central role of a "defective conscience" came to be appreciated. By the 20th century, these individuals would be called *sociopaths* or said to suffer from *antisocial personality disorder*, two terms that are still used interchangeably with psychopathy in some circles, while in others are considered distinct but related conditions.

The psychopath does not merely repress feelings of anxiety and guilt or fail to experience them appropriately; instead, he or she lacks a fundamental understanding of what these things are. When asked a question such as "What does remorse feel like?" for instance, the typical psychopath will become irritated, deflect the question, or attempt to change the subject. The following response from a psychopathic rapist, asked why he didn't empathize with his victims, shows just how distanced such a person can be from normal human emotion:

"They are frightened, right? But, you see, I don't really understand it. I've been frightened myself, and it wasn't unpleasant." –Hare, *Without Conscience: The Disturbing World of the Psychopaths Among Us*

Arriving at a disaster scene, a psychopath would most likely gather to watch with the rest of the crowd. He might even lend assistance if he perceived no threat to his own safety. But he would feel none of the panic, shock, or horror of the other onlookers—his interest would fall more on the reactions of the victims and of the crowd. He would not be repulsed by any carnage on display, except perhaps in the same sense as serial killer Paul Bernardo when he described cutting up one of his victims' bodies as "the most disgusting thing he had ever done." He was referring to the mess it made.

Despite this emotional deficiency, most psychopaths learn to mimic the appearance of normal emotion well enough to fit into ordinary society, not unlike the way that the hearing impaired or illiterate learn to use other cues to compensate for their disabilities. As Hare describes it, psychopaths "know the words but not the music." One might imagine that such a false and superficial front would be easily penetrated, but such is rarely the case, probably because of the assumption we all tend to make that others think and feel essentially the same way as ourselves. Differences in culture, gender, personality, and social status all create empathy gaps that can seem almost unfathomable, but none of these is as fundamental a divide as the one that exists between an individual with a conscience and one without. The psychopath's psychology is so profoundly alien to most people that we are unable to comprehend their motives, or recognize one when we see one. Naturally, the industrious psychopath will find this to his advantage.

Some psychologists go so far as to label the psychopath "a different kind of human" altogether. Psychopathy has an environmental component like nearly all aspects of personal psychology, but its source is rooted firmly in biology. This has caused some researchers to suspect that the condition isn't a "disorder" at all, but an adaptive trait. In a civilization made up primarily of law-abiding citizenry, the theory goes, an evolutionary niche opens up for a minority who would exploit the trusting masses.

This hypothesis is supported by the apparent success many psychopaths find within society. The majority of these individuals are not violent criminals; indeed, those that turn to crime are generally considered "unsuccessful psychopaths" due to their failure to blend into society. Those who do succeed can do so spectacularly. For instance, while it may sound like a cynical joke, it's a fact that psychopaths have a clear advantage in fields such as law, business, and politics. They have higher IQs on average than the general population. They take risks and aren't fazed by failures. They know how to charm and manipulate. They're ruthless. It could even be argued that the criteria used by corporations to find effective managers actually select specifically for psychopathic traits: characteristics such as charisma, self-centeredness, confidence, and dominance are highly correlated with the psychopathic personality, yet also highly sought after in potential leaders. It was not until recent years—in the wake of some well-publicized scandals involving corporate psychopaths—that many corporations started to reconsider these promotion policies. After all, psychopaths are interested only in their own gain, and trouble is inevitable when their interests begin to conflict with those of the company. This was the case at Enron, and again at WorldCom—and Sunbeam CEO Al Dunlap, besides doctoring the books and losing his company millions of dollars, would allegedly leave his wife at home without access to food or money for days at a time.

Hermann Goering

The thought of these people wearing suits and working a 9-5 job conflicts with most people's image of psychopaths gleaned from films like *The Godfather* and *The Silence of the Lambs*. But it shouldn't be surprising. A lack of empathy does not necessarily imply a desire to do

106

harm—that comes from sadism and tendencies toward violence, traits which have only a small correlation with psychopathy. When all three come together in one individual, of course, the result is catastrophic. Ted Bundy and Paul Bernardo are extreme examples of such a combination.

"Do I feel bad when I hurt someone? Yeah, sometimes. But mostly it's just like... uh... (laughs). I mean, how did you feel the last time you squashed a fly?" –Unnamed rapist/kidnapper

If psychopaths often appear where we don't expect them, neither does the clinical term always apply where we think it might. Nazi Luftwaffe chief Hermann Goering is thought to have met the diagnostic criteria, but Hitler's own behavior was frequently inconsistent with that of a psychopath. Columbine killer Eric Harris fit the description, but his accomplice Dylan Klebold did not. [In total, 50% of the violent offenders qualify as psychopathic but statistics have shown that 8:10 have behaviors of ASPD], and the difference from the general population is readily apparent to those who know them well. Even the most hardened of normal offenders can find their psychopathic cellmates unnerving.

The same discovery awaits most anyone who becomes close to such an individual. In romantic relationships, a psychopath may be charming and affectionate just long enough to establish intimacy with a partner, and then suddenly become abusive, unfaithful, and manipulative. The bewildered partner might turn to friends and family with their story, only to be met with disbelief—how could the warm, outgoing individual everyone has come to know possibly be guilty of these acts? All too often, the abused partner blames the situation on themselves, and comes out of the relationship emotionally destroyed.

But from a comfortable distance, the impression given off by a psychopath is often highly positive. The same absence of inhibitions and honesty that makes psychopaths so dangerous also gives them unusual powers of charisma through self-confidence and fabricated flattery. The aforementioned Sunbeam CEO Al Dunlap was a legend in business circles—"a corporate god," some called him—precisely for his ruthless, results-oriented business style and in-your-face, furniture-hurling personality. In social circles, psychopaths are often the most popular friends among members of both sexes. And strikingly, in entertainment media such as films and books, it's not just the villains who tend to have psychopathic personalities—it's the heroes, too.

One doesn't have to look far to find examples of this kind of protagonist. James Bond, the promiscuous, daring secret agent who can ski down a mountainside while being chased by armed attackers without breaking a sweat, is a textbook case. Frank Abagnale Jr., the charming con-man on whom the recent book and film *Catch Me if You Can* were based, is another highly likely candidate. And nearly every character played by action stars such as Arnold Schwarzenegger and Sylvester Stallone—the ones who vow revenge on an enemy and rampage about while coolly spouting one-liners—would qualify for a diagnosis.

"I wouldn't be here if my parents had come across when I needed them," he ['Terry,' imprisoned bank robber] said. "What kind of parents would let their son rot in a place like this?" Asked about his children, he replied, "I've never seen them. I think they were given up for adoption. How the hell should I know?" – Hare, *Without Conscience: The Disturbing World of the Psychopaths Among Us*

The reasons we look up to these conscience impaired people are unclear. Recent Bond film *Casino Royale* didn't shy away from acknowledging Bond's psychopathic tendencies. Most likely it has something to do with the confidence they exude, the ease they seem to feel in any situation—a trait that comes easily in someone essentially incapable of fear or anxiety. Maybe we're easily suckered in by their natural glibness and charm. Or maybe on some level we envy the freedom they have, with no burden of conscience or emotion.

The psychopaths, for their part, will never know things any other way. Most experts agree that the condition is permanent and completely untreatable. It's been theorized that their situation is the result of a kind of inherited learning disorder: without dread or anxiety to deter them, psychopaths are unable to make the associations between behavior and punishment that make up the building blocks of a normal conscience. That being the case, it is questionable whether a description such as "evil"—which is not uncommon in both the popular and scientific literature—can really be applied to individuals incapable of understanding what it means.

But to those who cross their paths, this may be small comfort.

PSYCHOPATHS AMONG US

Dr. Robert Hare claims there are 300,000 psychopaths in Canada, but that only a tiny fraction are violent offenders like Paul Bernardo and Clifford Olsen. Who are the rest? Take a look around

By Robert Hercz

"Psychopath! psychopath!" I'm alone in my living room and I'm yelling at my TV. "Forget rehabilitation -- that guy is a psychopath."

Ever since I visited Dr. Robert Hare in Vancouver, I can see them, the psychopaths. It's pretty easy, once you know how to look. I'm watching a documentary about an American prison trying to rehabilitate teen murderers. They're using an emotionally intense kind of group therapy, and I can see, as plain as day, that one of the inmates is a psychopath. He tries, but he can't muster a convincing breakdown, can't fake any feeling for his dead victims. He's learned the words, as Bob Hare would put it, but not the music.

The incredible thing, the reason I'm yelling, is that no one in this documentary -- the therapists, the warden, the omniscient narrator -- seems to know the word "psychopath." It is never uttered, yet it changes everything. A psychopath can never be made to feel the horror of murder. Weeks of intense therapy, which are producing real breakthroughs in the other youths, will probably make a psychopath more likely to reoffend. Psychopaths are not like the rest of us, and everyone who studies them agrees they should not be treated as if they were.

I think of Bob Hare, who's in New Orleans receiving yet another award, and wonder if he's watching the same show in his hotel room and feeling the same frustration. A lifetime spent looking into the heads of psychopaths has made the slight, slightly anxious emeritus professor of psychology at the University of British Columbia the world's best-known expert on the species. Hare hasn't merely changed our understanding of psychopaths. It would be more accurate to say he has created it.

The condition itself has been recognized for centuries, wearing evocative labels such as "madness without delirium" and "moral insanity" until the late 1800s, when "psychopath" was coined by a German clinician. But the term (and its 1930s synonym, sociopath) had always been a sort of catch-all, widely and loosely applied to criminals who seemed violent and unstable. Even into the mid-1970s, almost 80 percent of convicted felons in the United States were being diagnosed as sociopaths. In 1980, Hare created a diagnostic tool called the Psychopathy Checklist, which, revised five years later, became known as the PCL-R. Popularly called "the Hare," the PCL-R measures psychopathy on a forty-point scale. Once it emerged, it was the first time in history that everyone who said "psychopath" was saying the same thing. For research in the field, it was like a starting gun.

But for Hare, it has turned out to be a Pandora's Box. Recently retired from teaching, his very last Ph.D. student about to leave the nest, Hare, sixty-eight, should be basking in professional accolades and enjoying his well-earned rest. But he isn't.

The PCL-R has slipped the confines of academe, and is being used and misused in ways that Hare never intended. In some of the places where it could do some good -- such as the prison in the TV documentary I was yelling at -- the idea of psychopathy goes unacknowledged, usually because it's politically incorrect to declare someone to be beyond rehabilitation. At the opposite extreme, there are cases in which Hare's work has been overloaded with political baggage of another sort, such as in the United States, where a high PCL-R score is used to support death-penalty arguments, and in England, where a debate is underway about whether some individuals with personality disorders (such as psychopaths) should be detained even if they haven't committed a crime.

So, after decades of labor in peaceful obscurity, Bob Hare has become a man with a suitcase, a passport, and a PowerPoint presentation, a reluctant celebrity at gatherings of judges, attorneys, prison administrators, psychologists, and police. His post-retirement mission is to be a good shepherd to his Psychopathy Checklist.

"I'm protecting it from erosion, from distortion. It could easily be compromised," he says. "I'm a scientist; I should just be doing basic research, but I'm being called on all the time to intervene and mediate."

And it's really just beginning. Psychopathy may prove to be as important a construct in this century as IQ was in the last (and just as susceptible to abuse), because, thanks to Hare, we now understand that the great majority of psychopaths are not violent criminals and never will be. Hundreds of thousands of psychopaths live and work and prey among us. Your boss, your boyfriend, your mother could be what Hare calls a "subclinical" psychopath, someone who leaves a path of destruction and pain without a single pang of conscience. Even more worrisome is the fact that, at this stage, no one -- not even Bob Hare -- is quite sure what to do about it.

Bob hare has to meet me in the lobby of the UBC psychology building, since he's not listed in the directory. He's had threats, by e-mail and in person. An ex-con showed up one day, angry that a friend of his had been declared a dangerous offender thanks to Hare's checklist. Other characters have appeared in his lab doorway, looking in and saying nothing.

We immediately find ourselves discussing the criminal du jour, the jet-setting French con man Christophe Rocancourt, notorious for passing himself off as a member of the Rockefeller family, who has just been arrested in Victoria.

"I'd sure as hell like to have a close look at him," Hare muses.

Like every scientist, Hare likes a good puzzle, and that was reason enough to make a career out of psychopaths. "These were particularly interesting human beings," he says. "Everything about them seemed to be paradoxical. They could do things that a lot of other people could not do" -- lie, steal, rape, murder -- "but they looked perfectly normal, and when you talked to them they seemed okay. It was a puzzle. I thought I'd try and unravel it."

Hare arrived at UBC in 1963, intending to follow up his doctoral research on punishment. Certain prisoners, it was rumored, didn't respond to punishment, and Hare went to the federal penitentiary in New Westminster, British Columbia, to find these extreme cases. (He found plenty. In his chilling 1993 book on psychopathy, *Without Conscience: The Disturbing World of the Psychopaths Among Us*, he quotes one specimen's memories: "My mother, the most beautiful person in the world. She was strong, she worked hard to take care of four kids. A beautiful person. I started stealing her jewelry when I was in the fifth grade. You know, I never really knew the bitch -- we went our separate ways.")

For his first paper, now a classic, Hare had his subjects watch a countdown timer. When it reached zero, they got a "harmless but painful" electric shock while an electrode taped to their fingers measured perspiration. Normal people would start sweating as the countdown proceeded, nervously anticipating the shock. Psychopaths didn't sweat. They didn't fear punishment -- which, presumably, also holds true outside the laboratory. In *Without Conscience*, he quotes a psychopathic rapist explaining why he finds it hard to empathize with his victims: "They are frightened, right? But, you see, I don't really understand it. I've been frightened myself, and it wasn't unpleasant."

In another Hare study, groups of letters were flashed to volunteers. Some of them were nonsense, some formed real words. The subject's job was to press a button whenever he recognized a real word, while Hare recorded response time and brain activity. Non-psychopaths respond faster and display more brain activity when processing emotionally loaded words such as "rape" or "cancer" than when they see neutral words such as "tree." With psychopaths, Hare found no difference. To them, "rape" and "tree" have the same emotional impact -- none.

Hare made another intriguing discovery by observing the hand gestures (called beats) people make while speaking. Research has shown that such gestures do more than add visual emphasis to our words (many people gesture while they're on the telephone, for example); it seems they actually help our brains find words. That's why the frequency of beats increases when someone is having trouble finding words, or is speaking a second language instead of his or her mother tongue. In a 1991 paper, Hare and his colleagues reported that psychopaths, especially when talking about things they should find emotional, such as their families, produce a higher frequency of beats than normal people. It's as if emotional language is a second language -- a foreign language, in effect -- to the psychopath.

Three decades of these studies, by Hare and others, has confirmed that psychopaths' brains work differently from ours, especially when processing emotion and language. Hare once illustrated this for Nicole Kidman, who had invited him to Hollywood to help her prepare for a role as a psychopath in <u>Malice</u>. How, she wondered, could she show the audience there was something fundamentally wrong with her character?

"I said, 'Here's a scene that you can use,'" Hare says. "'You're walking down a street and there's an accident. A car has hit a child in the crosswalk. A crowd of people gather round. You walk up, the child's lying on the ground and there's blood running all over the place. You get a little blood on your shoes and you look down and say, "Oh shit." You look over at the child, kind of interested, but you're not repelled or horrified. You're just interested. Then you look at the mother, and you're really fascinated by the mother, who's emoting, crying out, doing all these different things. After a few minutes you turn away and go back to your house. You go into the bathroom and practice mimicking the facial expressions of the mother.' " He then pauses and says, "That's the psychopath: somebody who doesn't understand what's going on emotionally, but understands that something important has happened."

Hare's research upset a lot of people. Until the psychopath came into focus, it was possible to believe that bad people were just good people with bad parents or childhood trauma and that, with care, you could talk them back into being good. Hare's research suggested that some people behaved badly even when there had been no early trauma. Moreover, since psychopaths' brains were in fundamental ways different from ours, talking them into being like us might not be easy. Indeed, to this day, no one has found a way to do so.

"Some of the things he was saying about these individuals, it was unheard of," says Dr. Steven Stein, a psychologist and ceo of Multi-Health Systems in Toronto, the publisher of the Psychopathy Checklist. "Nobody believed him thirty years ago, but Bob hasn't wavered, and now everyone's where he is. Everyone's come full circle, except a small group who believe it's bad upbringing, family poverty, those kinds of factors, even though scientific evidence has shown that's not the case. There are wealthy psychopaths who've done horrendous things, and they were brought up in wonderful families."

"There's still a lot of opposition -- some criminologists, sociologists, and psychologists don't like psychopathy at all," Hare says. "I can spend the entire day going through the literature -- it's overwhelming, and unless you're semi-brain-dead you're stunned by it -- but a lot of people come out of there and say, 'So what? Psychopathy is a mythological construct.' They have political and social agendas: 'People are inherently good,' they say. 'Just give them a hug, a puppy dog, and a musical instrument and they're all going to be okay.' "

If Hare sounds a little bitter, it's because a decade ago, Correctional Service of Canada asked him to design a treatment program for psychopaths, but just after he submitted the plan in 1992, there were personnel changes at the top of CSC. The new team had a different agenda, which Hare summarizes as, "We don't believe in the badness of people." His plan sank without a trace.

By the late 1970s, after fifteen years in the business, Bob Hare knew what he was looking for when it came to psychopaths. They exhibit a cluster of distinctive personality traits, the most significant of which is an utter lack of conscience. They also have huge egos, short tempers, and an appetite for excitement -- a dangerous mix. In a typical prison population, about 20 percent of the inmates satisfy the Hare definition of a psychopath, but they are responsible for over half of all violent crime.

The research community, Hare realized, lacked a standard definition. "I found that we were all talking a different language, we were on different diagnostic pages, and I decided that we had to have some common instrument," he says. "The PCL-R was really designed to make it easier to publish articles and to let journal editors and reviewers know what I meant by psychopathy."

The Psychopathy Checklist consists of a set of forms and a manual that describes in detail how to score a subject in twenty categories that define psychopathy. Is he (or, more rarely, she) glib and superficially charming, callous and without empathy? Does he have a grandiose sense of self worth, shallow emotions, a lack of remorse or guilt? Is he impulsive, irresponsible, and promiscuous? Did he have behavioral problems early in life? The information for each category must be carefully drawn from documents such as court transcripts, police reports, psychologists' reports, and victim-impact statements, and not solely from an interview, since psychopaths are superb liars ("pathological lying" and "conning/manipulative" are PCL-R categories). A prisoner may claim to love his family, for example, while his records show no visits or phone calls.

For each item, assessors -- psychologists or psychiatrists -- assign a score of zero (the item doesn't apply), one (the item applies in some respects), or two (the item applies in most respects). The maximum possible score is forty, and the boundary for clinical psychopathy hovers around thirty. Last year, the average score for all incarcerated male offenders in North America was 23.3. Hare guesses his own score would be about four or five.

In 1980, Hare's initial checklist began circulating in the research community, and it quickly became the standard. At last count nearly 500 papers and 150 doctoral dissertations had been based on it.

It's also found practical applications in police-squad rooms. Soon after he delivered a keynote speech at a conference for homicide detectives and prosecuting attorneys in Seattle three years ago, Hare got a letter thanking him for helping solve a series of homicides. The police had a suspect nailed for a couple of murders, but believed he was responsible for others. They were using the usual strategy to get a confession, telling him, 'Think how much better you'll feel, think of the families left behind,' and so on. After they'd heard Hare speak they realized they were dealing with a psychopath, someone who could feel neither guilt nor sorrow. They changed their interrogation tactic to, "So you murdered a couple of prostitutes. That's minor-league compared to Bundy or Gacy." The appeal to the psychopath's grandiosity worked. He didn't just confess to his other crimes, he bragged about them.

The most startling finding to emerge from Hare's work is that the popular image of the psychopath as a remorseless, smiling killer -- Paul Bernardo, Clifford Olson, John Wayne Gacy -- while not wrong, is incomplete. Yes, almost all serial killers, and most of Canada's dangerous offenders, are psychopaths, but violent criminals are just a tiny fraction of the psychopaths around us. Hare estimates that 1 percent of the population -- 300,000 people in Canada -- are psychopaths.

He calls them "subclinical" psychopaths. They're the charming predators who, unable to form real emotional bonds, find and use vulnerable women for sex and money (and inevitably abandon them). They're the con men like Christophe Rocancourt, and they're the stockbrokers and promoters who caused Forbes magazine to call the Vancouver Stock Exchange (now part of the Canadian Venture Exchange) the scam capital of the world. (Hare has said that if he couldn't study psychopaths in prisons, the Vancouver Stock Exchange would have been his second choice.) A significant proportion of persistent wife beaters, and people who have unprotected sex despite carrying the AIDS virus, are psychopaths. Psychopaths can be found in legislatures, hospitals, and used-car lots. They're your neighbor, your boss, and your blind date. Because they have no conscience, they're natural predators. If you didn't have a conscience, you'd be one too.

Psychopaths love chaos and hate rules, so they're comfortable in the fast-moving modern corporation. Dr. Paul Babiak, an industrial-organizational psychologist based near New York City, is in the process of writing a book with Bob Hare called *When Psychopaths Go to Work: Cons, Bullies and the Puppetmaster.* The subtitle refers to the three broad classes of psychopaths Babiak has encountered in the workplace.

"The con man works one-on-one," says Babiak. "They'll go after a woman, marry her, take her money, then move on and marry someone else. The puppet master would manipulate somebody to get at someone else. This type is more powerful because they're hidden." Babiak says psychopaths have three motivations: thrill-seeking, the pathological desire to win, and the inclination to hurt people. "They'll jump on any opportunity that allows them to do those things," he says. "If something better comes along, they'll drop you and move on."

How can you tell if your boss is a psychopath? It's not easy, says Babiak. "They have traits similar to ideal leaders. You would expect an ideal leader to be narcissistic, self-centered, dominant, very assertive, maybe to the point of being aggressive. Those things can easily be mistaken for the aggression and bullying that a psychopath would demonstrate. The ability to get people to follow you is a leadership trait, but being charismatic to the point of manipulating people is a psychopathic trait. They can sometimes be confused."

Once inside a company, psychopaths can be hard to excise. Babiak tells of a salesperson and psychopath -- call him John -- who was performing badly but not suffering for it. John was managing his boss -- flattering him, taking him out for drinks, flying to his side when he was in trouble. In return, his boss covered for him by hiding John's poor performance. The arrangement lasted until John's boss was moved. When his replacement called John to task for his abysmal sales numbers, John was a step ahead.

He'd already gone to the company president with a set of facts he used to argue that his new boss, and not he, should be fired. But he made a crucial mistake. "It was actually stolen data," Babiak says. "The only way [John] could have obtained it would be for him to have gone into a file into which no one was supposed to go. That seemed to be enough, and he was fired rather than the boss. Even so, in the end, he walked out with a company car, a bag of money, and a good reference."

"A lot of white-collar criminals are psychopaths," says Bob Hare. "But they flourish because the characteristics that define the disorder are actually valued. When they get caught, what happens? A slap on the wrist, a six-month ban from trading, and don't give us the $100 million back. I've always looked at white-collar crime as being as bad or worse than some of the physically violent crimes that are committed."

The best way to protect the workplace is not to hire psychopaths in the first place. That means training interviewers so they're less likely to be manipulated and conned. It means checking resumes' for lies and distortions, and it means following up references.

Paul Babiak says he's "not comfortable" with one researcher's estimate that one in ten executives is a psychopath, but he has noticed that they are attracted to positions of power. When he describes employees such as John to other executives, they know exactly whom he's talking about. "I was talking to a group of human-resources executives yesterday," says Babiak, "and every one of them said, you know, I think I've got somebody like that."

By now, you're probably thinking the same thing. The number of psychopaths in society is about the same as the number of schizophrenics, but unlike schizophrenics, psychopaths aren't loners. That means most of us have met or will meet one. Hare gets dozens of letters and e-mail messages every month from people who say they recognize someone they know while reading *Without Conscience*. They go on to describe a brother, a sister, a husband. "'Please help my seventeen-year-old son. . . .'" Hare reads aloud from one such missive. "It's a heart-wrenching letter, but what can I do? I'm not a clinician. I have hundreds of these things, and some of them are thirty or forty pages long."

Hare's book opened my eyes, too. Reading it, I realized that I might have known a psychopath, Jonathan, at the computer company where I worked in London, England, over twenty years ago. He was charming and confident, and from the moment he arrived he was on excellent terms with the executive inner circle. Jonathan had big plans and promised me that I was a big part of them. One night when I was alone in the office, Jonathan appeared, accompanied by what anyone should have recognized as two prostitutes. "These are two high-ranking staff from the Ministry of Defense," he said without missing a beat. "We're going over the details of a contract, which I'm afraid is classified top secret. You'll have to leave the building." His voice and eyes were absolutely persuasive and I complied. A few weeks later Jonathan was arrested. He had embezzled tens of thousands of pounds from the small firm, used the company as a mailing address for a marijuana importing business he was running on the side, and robbed the apartment of the company's owner, who was letting him stay there temporarily.

Like everyone who has been suckered by a psychopath -- and Bob Hare includes himself and many of his graduate students (who have been trained to spot them) in that list -- I'm ashamed that I fell for Jonathan. But he was brilliant, charismatic, and audacious. He radiated money and power (though in fact he had neither), while his real self -- manipulative, lying, parasitic, and irresponsible -- was just far enough under his surface to be invisible. Or was it? Maybe I didn't know how to look, or maybe I didn't really want to.

I saw his name in the news again recently. "A con man tricked top sports car makers Lotus into lending him a $70,000 model then he stole and drove it 6,000 miles across Europe, a court heard," the story began.

Knowing Jonathan is probably a psychopath makes me feel better. It's an explanation.

But away from the workplace, back in the world of the criminally violent psychopath, Hare's checklist has become broadly known, so broadly known, in fact, that it is now a constant source of concern for him. "People are misusing it, and they're misusing it in really strange ways," Hare says. "There are lots of clinicians who don't even have a manual. All they've seen is an article with the twenty items -- promiscuity, impulsiveness, and so forth -- listed."

In court, assessments of the same person done by defense and prosecution "experts" have varied by as much as twenty points. Such drastic differences are almost certainly the result of bias or incompetence, since research on the PCL-R itself has shown it has high "inter-rater reliability" (consistent results when a subject is assessed by more than one qualified assessor). In one court case, it was used to label a thirteen-year-old a psychopath, even though the

PCL-R test is only meant to be used to rate adults with criminal histories. The test should be administered only by mental health professionals (like all such psychological instruments, it is only for sale to those with credentials), but a social worker once used the PCL-R in testimony in a death-penalty case -- not because she was qualified but because she thought it was "interesting."

It shouldn't be used in death-penalty cases at all, Hare says, but U.S. Federal District Courts have ruled it admissible because it meets scientific standards.

"Bob and others like myself are saying it doesn't meet the ethical standards," says Dr. Henry Richards, a psychopathy researcher at the University of Washington. "A psychological instrument and diagnosis should not be a determinant of whether someone gets the death sentence. That's more of an ethical and political decision."

And into the ethical and political realm -- the realm of extrapolation, of speculation, of opinion -- Hare will not step. He's been asked to be a guest on *Oprah* (twice), *60 Minutes*, and *Larry King Live*. Oprah wanted him alongside a psychopath and his victim. "I said, 'This is a circus,' " Hare says. "I couldn't do that." *60 Minutes* also wanted to "make it sexy" by throwing real live psychopaths into the mix. *Larry King Live* phoned him at home while O. J. Simpson was rolling down the freeway in his white Bronco. Hare says no every time (while his publisher gently weeps).

Even in his particular area, Hare is unfailingly circumspect. Asked if he thinks there will ever be a cure for psychopathy -- a drug, an operation -- Hare steps back and examines the question. "The psychopath will say 'A cure for what?' I don't feel comfortable calling it a disease. Much of their behavior, even the neurobiological patterns we observe, could be because they're using different strategies to get around the world. These strategies don't have to involve faulty wiring, just different wiring."

Are these people qualitatively different from us? "I would think yes," says Hare. "Do they form a discrete taxon or category? I would say probably -- the evidence is suggesting that. But does this mean that's because they have a broken motor? I don't know. It could be a natural variation." True saints, completely selfless individuals, are rare and unnatural too, he points out, but we don't talk about their being diseased.

Psychopathy research is raising more questions than it can answer, and many of them are leading to moral and ethical quagmires. For example: the PCL-R has turned out to be the best single predictor of recidivism that has ever existed; an offender with a high PCL-R score is three or four times more likely to reoffend than someone with a low score. Should a high PCL-R score, then, be sufficient grounds for denying parole? Or perhaps a psychopathy test could be used to prevent crime by screening individuals or groups at high risk -- for example, when police get a frantic "My boyfriend says he'll kill me" call, or when a teacher reports a student threatening to commit violence. Should society institutionalize psychopaths, even if they haven't broken the law?

The United Kingdom, partly in response to the 1993 abduction and murder of two-year-old James Bulger by two ten-year-olds, and partly in response to PCL-R data, is in the process of creating a new legal classification called Dangerous and Severe Personality Disorder (DSPD). As it stands, the government proposes to allow authorities to detain people declared DSPD, even if they have not committed a crime. (Sample text from one of the Web sites that have sprung up in response: "I was diagnosed with an untreatable personality disorder by a doctor who saw me for ten minutes, he later claimed I was a psychopath. . . . Please don't let them do this to me; don't let them do it to anybody. I'm not a danger to the public, nor are most mentally ill people.")

Hare is a consultant on the DSPD project, and finds the potential for abuse of power horrifying. So do scientists such as Dr. Richard Tees, head of psychology at UBC, a colleague of Hare's since 1965. "I am concerned about our political masters deciding that the PCL-R is the silver bullet that's going to fix everything," he says. "We'll let people out [of prison] on the basis of scores on this, and we'll put them in. And we'll take children who do badly on some version of this and segregate them or something. It wasn't designed to do any of these things. The problems that politicians are trying to solve are fundamentally more complicated than the one that Bob has solved."

So many of these awkward questions would vanish if only there were a functioning treatment program for psychopathy. But there isn't. In fact, several studies have shown that existing treatment makes criminal psychopaths worse. In one, psychopaths who underwent social-skills and anger-management training before release had an 82 percent reconviction rate. Psychopaths who didn't take the program had a 59 percent reconviction rate. Conventional psychotherapy starts with the assumption that a patient wants to change, but psychopaths are usually perfectly happy as they are. They enroll in such programs to improve their chances of parole. "These guys learn the words but not the music," Hare says. "They can repeat all the psychiatric jargon -- 'I feel remorse,' they talk about the offence cycle -- but these are words, hollow words."

Hare has co-developed a new treatment program specifically for violent psychopaths, using what he knows about the psychopathic personality. The idea is to encourage them to be better by appealing not to their (non-existent) altruism but to their (abundant) self-interest.

"It's not designed to change personality, but to modify behavior by, among other things, convincing them that there are ways they can get what they want without harming others," Hare explains. The program will try to make them understand that violence is bad, not for society, but for the psychopath himself. (Look where it got you: jail.) A similar program will soon be put in place for psychopathic offenders in the UK.

"The irony is that Canada could have had this all set up and they could have been leaders in the world. But they dropped the ball completely," Hare says, referring to his decade-old treatment proposal, sitting on a shelf somewhere within Corrections Canada.

Even if Hare's treatment program works, it will only address the violent minority of psychopaths. What about the majority, the subclinical psychopaths milling all around us? At the moment, the only thing Hare and his colleagues can offer is self-protection through self-education. Know your own weaknesses, they advise, because the psychopath will find and use them. Learn to recognize the psychopath, they tell us, before adding that even experts are regularly taken in.

After thirty-five years of work, Bob Hare has brought us to the stage where we know what psychopathy is, how much damage psychopaths do, and even how to identify them. But we don't know how to treat them or protect the population from them. The real work is just beginning. Solving the puzzle of the psychopath is an invigorating prospect -- if you're a scientist. Perhaps the rest of us can be forgiven for our impatience to see the whole thing come to an end.

Serial killers and Animal Abuse

Posted by thebosun on August 1, 2006

The **Phoenix Police Department** has been investigating animal abuse as part of their ongoing investigations. A little historical date on notorious serial killers linked to animal abuse in the United States:

As a child, serial killer and rapist **Ted Bundy**—ultimately convicted of two killings but suspected of murdering more than 40 women—witnessed his father's **violence toward animals**, and he himself subsequently tortured animals.

Earl Kenneth Shriner, who raped and stabbed a 7-year-old boy, was known in his neighborhood for **hanging cats** and **torturing dogs**.

David Berkowitz (a.k.a. "Son of Sam"), pled guilty to 13 murders and attempted murder charges, **shot a neighbor's Labrador retriever.**

Brenda Spencer, who opened fire at a California school, killing two children and injuring nine others, had **repeatedly abused cats** and **dogs**, often **setting their tails on fire**.

Serial killer and cannibal **Jeffrey Dahmer** impaled the **heads of dogs** and **cats on sticks**.

A very informative site on serial criminals and animal abuse is http://www.helpinganimals.com/ga_humanAbuse.asp

Violent acts toward animals have long been recognized as indicators of a dangerous psychopathy that does not confine itself to animals. "Anyone who has accustomed himself to regard the life of any living creature as worthless is in danger of arriving also at the idea of worthless human lives," wrote humanitarian Dr. Albert Schweitzer. "Murderers ... very often start out by killing and torturing animals as kids," according to Robert K. Ressler, who developed profiles of serial killers for the Federal Bureau of Investigation (FBI). Studies have now convinced sociologists, lawmakers, and the courts that acts of cruelty toward animals deserve our attention. They can be the first sign of a violent pathology that includes human victims.

Animal abuse is not just the result of a minor personality flaw in the abuser but rather a symptom of a deep mental disturbance. Research in psychology and criminology shows that people who commit acts of cruelty toward animals don't stop there; many of them move on to their fellow humans.

The FBI has found that a history of cruelty to animals is one of the traits that regularly appear in its computer records of serial rapists and murderers, and the standard diagnostic and treatment manual for psychiatric and emotional disorders lists cruelty to animals as a diagnostic criterion for conduct disorders.

A study conducted by Northeastern University and the Massachusetts SPCA found that people who abuse animals are five times more likely to commit violent crimes against humans. The majority of inmates scheduled to be executed for murder at California's San Quentin penitentiary "practiced" their crimes on animals, according to the warden.

School Shooters Share Violent Past

April 1999 - Littleton, Colo. **Eric Harris** and **Dylan Klebold** shot to death 12 fellow students and a teacher and injured more than 20 others. Both teens had reportedly boasted about **mutilating animals**.

May 1998/Springfield, Ore. **Kip Kinkel,** 15, killed his parents and opened fire in his high school cafeteria, killing two and injuring 22 others. He had a history of animal abuse and torture, having boasted about **blowing up a cow** and **killing cats, chipmunks,** and **squirrels** by putting lit firecrackers in their mouths.

March 1998/Jonesboro, Ark. **Mitchell Johnson**, 13, and **Andrew Golden,** 11, pulled their school's fire alarm and then shot and killed four classmates and a teacher. Golden reportedly used to **shoot dogs** "all the time with a .22."

December 1997/West Paducah, Ky. **Michael Carneal**, 14, shot and killed three students during a school prayer meeting. Carneal had been heard talking about **throwing a cat into a bonfire**.

October 1997/Pearl, Miss. **Luke Woodham**, 16, shot and killed two of his classmates and injured seven others after stabbing his mother to death. Woodham's journal revealed that, in a moment of "true beauty," he and a friend had **beaten, burned,** and **tortured his own dog**, Sparkle, to death.

According to Charles Bahn a forensic psychologist at the John Jay College of Criminal Justice in New York, serial predators are rare.

To have two on the loose at the same time is almost unheard of. Bahn did not believe the killers were directly competing with one another; however, they appear to be "influencing" each other.

Said Bahn, "When they are reading about the attacks in the news the feeling is that the other person is satisfying the hunger - a satisfaction they themselves are not getting." It appears that we have a couple very sick individuals in Phoenix who are lashing out at with opportunity to kill humans and animals. Should the people of Phoenix tremble in fear, heck no. Sounds like the people of Phoenix are being very proactive about the killers in their city. The citizens of Phoenix are going about their daily routines, banding together to keep a watchful eye over their city. It is a matter of time before the serial killers make a mistake and get caught. One can only hope that they are caught soon before they murder another innocent victim.

This entry was posted on August 1, 2006

The Cruelty Connection

Childhood cruelty to animals is a strong warning of future violence to humans:

What Serial Shooters and Private Steven Green Have in Common
by Peta.org on Sept. 29, 2006

Every time a serial killer or perpetrator of a particularly violent crime is apprehended, you can bet that, eventually, it will be revealed that the killer **"practiced" his crimes on animals**.

In the case of **Steven D. Green**, the former soldier accused of orchestrating the murder of a 14-year-old Iraqi girl and her family, testimony at his alleged co-conspirators? recent court-martial hearing revealed that Green had previously set a puppy on fire and thrown the animal off a roof. Chillingly, the young girl who was raped and killed was also set on fire.

In Arizona, accused serial shooters **Samuel John Dieteman** and **Dale S. Hausner** allegedly shot nearly a dozen animals as well as 17 people during their 2-month-long killing spree in and around Phoenix. I believe that, as officials delve into their backgrounds, more cases of cruelty to animals will be unearthed, as they have been in virtually every serial killer case.

"There is not much of a leap between hurting poor defenseless animals to inflicting terror on vulnerable unsuspecting humans", commented Phoenix's KTVK-TV anchor Frank Camacho, about the Serial Shooter case. Catching an animal abuser early is one reason why the Humane Society has a team of investigators on staff who handle nothing but animal cruelty cases.?

Legislators and law enforcement authorities need to be aware of the **link between cruelty to animals and violent crimes against humans**. They need to act swiftly when people abuse animals. Fortunately, cruelty to animals is now a felony in 42 states. Animal cruelty task forces have been set up in several jurisdictions, including Delaware, New Hampshire, Vermont County, S.C., Marion County, Ind., Knox County, Tenn., Los Angeles, Calif. and Phoenix, Az

In November, 2005, the Los Angeles task force announced its first felony conviction, that of a gang member who scalded a puppy and shot her with a stun gun as a means of intimidating his girlfriend. At a press conference announcing the conviction, L.A. Mayor Antonio Villaraigosa said, *"When we protect animals, we are protecting ourselves, by protecting our communities."*

Mr. Villaraigosa is correct. Consider that **Carroll Edward Cole**, who was executed for five of the 35 murders of which he was accused, said his first act of violence was to strangle a puppy. **Albert DeSalvo**, the "Boston Strangler" **trapped dogs** and **cats** in orange crates and **shot** them with arrows. During the sentencing hearing of "BTK" killer Dennis Rader, it was revealed that, as a youth, Rader had **captured stray cats** and **dogs** and **strangled them**. However the crimes he later reenacted on humans. Convicted serial shooter **Lee Boyd Malvo** honed his marksmanship skills **shooting cats** with a slingshot. "Son of Sam" **David Berkowitz**, **Ted Bundy**, and **Jeffrey Dahmer** also **tortured and killed animals**. All of the kids involved in the deadly shootings at Columbine and other schools **killed animals** before attacking their classmates.

It is vital that violent attacks on animals, especially among young people, are taken seriously. Perhaps, if **Steven Greens** cruelty to animals had been reported and he had gotten the treatment he so desperately needs, Iraq would not be mourning the loss of a girl and her family who appear to have died at the hands of the young men who were charged with protecting them.

Alisa Mullins is Senior Writer for People for the Ethical Treatment of Animals, 501 Front St., Norfolk, VA 23510; www.Peta.org.

Dr. Phil's 14 Characteristics of a Serial Killer

Could you be raising a criminal? Acts of violence don't come out of nowhere, and every parent should be aware of the clues along the way. For the most violent of criminals, there are warning signs that often start in childhood. Below is a list of the **14 most common traits of serial killers**.

1. Over 90% of serial killers are male.

2. They tend to be intelligent, with IQ's in the "bright normal" range.

3. They do poorly in school, have trouble holding down jobs, and often work as unskilled laborers.

4. They tend to come from markedly unstable families.

5. As children, they are abandoned by their fathers and raised by domineering mothers.

6. Their families often have criminal, psychiatric and alcoholic histories.

7. They hate their fathers and mothers.

8. They are commonly abused as children — psychologically, physically and sexually. Often the abuse is by a family member.

9. Many serial killers spend time in institutions as children and have

records of early psychiatric problems.

10. They have high rates of suicide attempts.

11. From an early age, many are intensely interested in voyeurism, fetishism, and sadomasochistic pornography.

12. Over 60% of serial killers wet their beds beyond the age of twelve.

13. Many serial killers are fascinated with fire starting.

14. They are involved with sadistic activity or torment of animals.

Source:Internal Association of Forensic Science, an article written by FBI Special Agent Robert K. Ressler

Human Abuse & Cruelty to Animals

Violent acts toward animals have long been recognized as indicators of a dangerous psychopathy that does not confine itself to animals. "Anyone who has accustomed himself to regard the life of any living creature as worthless is in danger of arriving also at the idea of worthless human lives," wrote humanitarian Dr. Albert Schweitzer. "Murderers … very often start out by killing and torturing animals as kids," according to Robert K. Ressler, who developed profiles of serial killers for the Federal Bureau of Investigation (FBI). Studies have now convinced sociologists, lawmakers, and the courts that acts of cruelty toward animals deserve our attention. They can be the first sign of a violent pathology that includes human victims.

Animal abuse is not just the result of a minor personality flaw in the abuser but rather a symptom of a deep mental disturbance. Research in psychology and criminology shows that people who commit acts of cruelty toward animals don't stop there; many of them move on to their fellow humans.

The FBI has found that a history of cruelty to animals is one of the traits that regularly appear in its computer records of serial rapists and murderers, and the standard diagnostic and treatment manual for psychiatric and emotional disorders lists cruelty to animals as a diagnostic criterion for conduct disorders.

A study conducted by Northeastern University and the Massachusetts SPCA found that people who abuse animals are five times more likely to commit violent crimes against humans. The majority of inmates scheduled to be executed for murder at California's San Quentin penitentiary "practiced" their crimes on animals, according to the warden, **www.HelpingAnimals.com**

ANIMAL CRUELTY AND INTERPERSONAL VIOLENCE

To animal lovers, violence against animals is cruel and unfathomable. To the rest of the world, it is 'just an animal'. Humans matter more. But aren't humans really the cruelest species of all? Most animals kill for food and territory, but humans kill also for sport, entertainment, fashion, and cosmetics! Many researchers have found that a history of animal violence indicates a high propensity for interpersonal violence. Simply, those who abuse animals usually move on to human victims. Although not all animal abusers become serial killer, most serial killers began their killing spree with animals. The difference is that those who do not learn that it is cruel and wrong. In any case, repeated and extreme violence indicates a serious psychological violence that requires immediate treatment.

The cause of animal violence, according to Mother Hildegard George, a child psychologist and nun, our culture of violence. This culture of violence conditions and sensitizes us to violence, and teaches us to discriminate. Against people different from us, and animals. Discrimination is dangerous because it gives us an excuse to exercise that propensity for violence embedded in us. It gives us an excuse to abuse, mistreat, and deny rights to those we discriminate against. This is evident in the slavery of Black people in America last century and early this century, abuse of the Jewish people in Nazi Germany in World War II, devaluation of women before this century, and world-wide abuse of animals to perpetuate the human race.

What we must do is to change our perceptions and open our eyes. After all, animals inhabited this world way before us. What right have we to abuse and enslave them to 'improve' our lives? Lawmakers must be made aware of this connection between animal cruelty and interpersonal violence, and laws changed to detect, rehabilitate or punish animal abusers. Humane education should be practiced in schools. Pets should be treated as members of the family, not as an inferior species. Children should be taught to respect all animals, then they will too respect all life. Right now, we should increase awareness of this connection between animal cruelty and interpersonal violence. Imagine if people were taught this fact, how many lives, animal and human, could have been saved.

Extrapolation of Prevalence Rate of Anti-Social Personality Disorder to Countries and Regions:

*The following attempts to show the **2004** prevalence rate for **Anti-Social Personality Disorder** to the populations of various countries & regions:*

Country/Region	Prevalence	Population Estimated Used
Anti-Social Personality Disorder in North America		
USA	6,166,763	293,655,405[1]
Canada	682,665	32,507,874[2]
Mexico	2,204,151	104,959,594[2]
Anti-Social Personality Disorder in Central America		
Belize	5,731	272,945[2]
Guatemala	299,892	14,280,596[2]
Nicaragua	112,554	5,359,759[2]
Anti-Social Personality Disorder in Caribbean		
Puerto Rico	81,857	3,897,960[2]
Anti-Social Personality Disorder in South America		
Brazil	3,866,123	184,101,109[2]
Chile	332,303	15,823,957[2]
Colombia	888,526	42,310,775[2]
Paraguay	130,018	6,191,368[2]
Peru	578,430	27,544,305[2]
Venezuela	525,365	25,017,387[2]
Anti-Social Personality Disorder in Northern Europe		
Denmark	113,681	5,413,392[2]
Finland	109,504	5,214,512[2]
Iceland	6,173	293,966[2]
Sweden	188,714	8,986,400[2]
Anti-Social Personality Disorder in Western Europe		
Britain / U.K.	1,265,684	60,270,708 for UK[2]
Belgium	217,313	10,348,276[2]
France	1,268,908	60,424,213[2]
Ireland	83,360	3,969,558[2]

Luxembourg	9,716	462,690[2]
Monaco	677	32,270[2]
Netherlands (Holland)	342,682	16,318,199[2]
United Kingdom	1,265,684	60,270,708[2]
Wales	61,277	2,918,000[2]
Anti-Social Personality Disorder in Central Europe		
Austria	171,669	8,174,762[2]
Czech Republic	26,169	1,0246,178[2]
Germany	1,730,916	82,424,609[2]
Hungary	210,679	10,032,375[2]
Liechtenstein	702	33,436[2]
Poland	811,153	38,626,349[2]
Slovakia	113,894	5,423,567[2]
Slovenia	42,240	2,011,473 [2]
Switzerland	156,468	7,450,867[2]
Anti-Social Personality Disorder in Eastern Europe		
Belarus	216,520	10,310,520[2]
Estonia	28,174	1,341,664[2]
Latvia	48,432	2,306,306[2]
Lithuania	75,765	3,607,899[2]
Russia	3,023,455	143,974,059[2]
Ukraine	1,002,373	47,732,079[2]
Anti-Social Personality Disorder in the Southwestern Europe		
Azerbaijan	165,236	7,868,385[2]
Georgia	98,571	4,693,892[2]
Portugal	221,007	10,524,145[2]
Spain	845,896	40,280,780[2]
Anti-Social Personality Disorder in Southern Europe		
Greece	223,598	10,647,529[2]
Italy	1,219,206	58,057,477[2]
Anti-Social Personality Disorder in the Southeastern Europe		
Albania	74,440	3,544,808[2]

Bosnia /Herzegovina	8,559	407,608[2]
Bulgaria	157,877	7,517,973[2]
Croatia	94,434	4,496,869[2]
Macedonia	42,841	2,040,085[2]
Romania	469,466	22,355,551[2]
Serbia / Montenegro	227,343	10,825,900[2]

Anti-Social Personality Disorder in Northern Asia

Mongolia	57,777	2,751,314[2]

Anti-Social Personality Disorder in Central Asia

Kazakhstan	318,017	15,143,704[2]
Tajikistan	147,242	7,011,556 [2]
Uzbekistan	554,618	26,410,416[2]

Anti-Social Personality Disorder in Eastern Asia

China	27,275,798	1,298,847,624[2]
Hong Kong s.a.r.	143,957	6,855,125[2]
Japan	2,673,992	127,333,002[2]
Macau s.a.r.	9,351	445,286[2]
North Korea	476,648	22,697,553[2]
South Korea	1,012,908	48,233,760[2]
Taiwan	477,746	22,749,838[2]

Anti-Social Personality Disorder in Southwestern Asia

Turkey	1,446,772	68,893,918[2]

Anti-Social Personality Disorder in Southern Asia

Afghanistan	598,787	28,513,677[2]
Bangladesh	2,968,149	141,340,476[2]
Bhutan	45,896	2,185,569[2]
India	22,366,481	1,065,070,607[2]
Pakistan	3,343,122	159,196,336[2]
Sri Lanka	418,008	19,905,165[2]

Anti-Social Personality Disorder in Southeastern Asia

East Timor	21,404	1,019,252[2]
Indonesia	5,007,511	238,452,952[2]

Laos	127,430	$6,068,117^2$
Malaysia	493,972	$23,522,482^2$
Philippines	1,811,075	$86,241,697^2$
Singapore	91,431	$4,353,893^2$
Thailand	1,362,175	$64,865,523^2$
Vietnam	1,735,918	$82,662,800^2$

Anti-Social Personality Disorder in the Middle East

Gaza strip	27,824	$1,324,991^2$
Iran	1,417,567	$67,503,205^2$
Iraq	532,868	$25,374,691^2$
Israel	130,179	$6,199,008^2$
Jordan	117,835	$5,611,202^2$
Kuwait	47,408	$2,257,549^2$
Lebanon	79,321	$3,777,218^2$
Saudi Arabia	541,714	$25,795,938^2$
Syria	378,354	$18,016,874^2$
United Arab Emrates	53,002	$2,523,915^2$
West Bank	48,535	$2,311,204^2$
Yemen	420,522	$20,024,867^2$

Anti-Social Personality Disorder in Northern Africa

Egypt	1,598,465	$76,117,421^2$
Libya	118,263	$5,631,585^2$
Sudan	822,111	$39,148,162^2$

Anti-Social Personality Disorder in Western Africa

Congo Brazzaville	62,958	$2,998,040^2$
Ghana	435,897	$20,757,032^2$
Liberia	71,203	$3,390,635^2$
Niger	238,571	$11,360,538^2$
Nigeria	372,757	$12,5750,356^2$
Senegal	227,895	$10,852,147^2$
Sierra Leone	123,561	$5,883,889^2$

133

Anti-Social Personality Disorder in Central Africa		
Central African Republic	78,592	$3,742,482^2$
Chad	200,309	$9,538,544^2$
Congo Kinshasa	1,224,657	$58,317,030^2$
Rwanda	173,012	$8,238,673^2$
Anti-Social Personality Disorder in Eastern Africa		
Ethiopia	1,498,067	$71,336,571^2$
Kenya	692,624	$32,982,109^2$
Somalia	174,396	$8,304,601^2$
Tanzania	757,486	$36,070,799^2$
Uganda	554,195	$26,390,258^2$
Anti-Social Personality Disorder in Southern Africa		
Angola	230,549	$10,978,552^2$
Botswana	34,423	$1,639,231^2$
South Africa	933,417	$44,448,470^2$
Swaziland	24,554	$1,169,241^2$
Zambia	231,539	$11,025,690^2$
Zimbabwe	77,109	$1,2671,860^2$
Anti-Social Personality Disorder in Oceania		
Australia	418,176	$19,913,144^2$
New Zealand	83,870	$3,993,817^2$
Papua New Guinea	113,825	$5,420,280^2$

US Census Bureau, Population Estimates, 2004 via www.WrongDiagnosis.com

Some Chilling Statistics

The U.S. Bureau of Statistics reported that in **1996** there were 9.1 million violent crimes in the United States.

A **1997** study by the MSPCA and Northeastern University found that **70%** of **animal abusers** had committed at least one other criminal offense and almost 40% had committed violent crimes against people.

A **1986** study reported that **48%** of **convicted rapists** and **30%** of **convicted child molesters** admitted perpetrating acts of animal cruelty in their childhood or adolescence.

A history of animal abuse was found in **25%** of **aggressive male criminals, 30%** of **convicted child molesters, 36%** of those who **assaulted women**, and **46%** of those convicted of **sexual homicide**.

In three surveys in women's shelters in Wisconsin and Utah in the 1990's, an average of **74% of pet-owning women** reported that a pet had been threatened, injured or killed by the abusers.

The Buffalo, NY police department found that **1/3 of the residences with animal abuse complaints** also had domestic violence complaints in 1998.

A Utah safe house found **20% delayed leaving** the abusive situation out of fear that their pet would be harmed. Data collected in Canada found almost **50%** delayed leaving.

The 1995 Utah survey also found that **children witnessed the animal abuse in over 60% of the cases** and **32%** of women reported that one or more of their children hurt or killed a pet.

A **1983** survey in New Jersey of families reported for child abuse found that in **88%** of the families at least one person had abused animals.

The New Jersey study also found that in **2/3** of these cases, the **abusive parent had injured** or **killed a pet** and in **1/3** of the cases, children were the animal abusers.

A study by the Royal SPCA in Great Britain found that **83% of families** with a history of animal abuse had also been identified by social service agencies as at-risk for child abuse or neglect.

Animal Cruelty, Serial Killers and Violence

The studies on this page reveal the prevalence of acts of animal **cruelty** among the most depraved and malicious criminals in society.

- Of the nine school shootings between 1996 and 1999, half of the shooters had histories of animal cruelty.

- The **largest** single survey to date of serial killers found:

  - 36 % committed animal cruelty as children
  - 46 % committed animal cruelty as adolescents
  - 36 % committed animal cruelty as adults.

- A **2003 study** found that of 354 serial killers profiled, 21% were known to have committed animal cruelty, although it is speculated that more might have committed unreported incidents of animal cruelty.

- A **Canadian Police study** found that 70 % of people arrested for animal cruelty had past records of other violent crimes, including homicide.

- Of **332 animal cruelty arrests** studied by the Chicago Police Department,

  - 70% had arrests on felony charges (including two homicides)
  - 86% had multiple arrests
  - 70% had narcotics charges (68 % were for sales or trafficking)
  - 65% had been charged with battery-related violent offenses
  - 27% had previous firearms charges
  - 13% had been arrested on sex crime charges
  - 59% were alleged gang members.

- A Massachusetts study of **153 animal abusers** found that within 10 years of their arrest, 70% were charged with other crimes:

  - 38% were violent crimes;
  - 44% were property crimes;

- 37% were drug offenses;
- 37% were charged with disorderly offenses.

An Australian study of **convicted animal abusers** found: 61.5 percent had been convicted for violent offenses against humans

- 17% had been convicted for sexual abuse
- 8% had been convicted for arson.

The Animal Abuse & Human Violence Connection

"One of the most dangerous things that can happen to a child is to kill or torture an animal and get away with it." -Anthropologist Margaret Mead

Until the past 20 years, the connection between violence against animals and violence against humans went unrecognized. Now a growing body of research has shown that people who abuse animals rarely stop there.

Increasingly, child protection and social service agencies, mental health professionals, and educators recognize that animal abuse is aggressive and antisocial behavior. It is also a reliable predictor of violence against people after a young abuser grows up.

Children learn about abuse by being its victim. They often fail to develop empathy, and without this key quality they cannot recognize their victims' pain. When they begin to "act out" their abuse trauma, children first target animals. As adults, they find new victims among the most vulnerable--children, partners, and the elderly.

Consider the following facts:

- The **FBI** sees animal cruelty as a predictor of violence against people and considers past animal abuse when profiling serial killers.
- National and state studies have established that from **71%** of **women seeking shelter** from abuse reported that their partners had threatened, injured or killed one or more family pets In assessing youth at risk of becoming violent, the U.S. Department of Justice stresses a history of animal abuse.

- More than **80%** of family members being treated for child abuse also had abused animals. In 2/3 of these cases, an abusive parent had killed or injured a pet. In one-third of the cases, a child victim continued the cycle of violence by abusing a pet.

A **1997** study by the Massachusetts Society for the Prevention of Cruelty to Animals and Northeastern University found that **70%** of animal abusers had committed at least one other crime. Almost 40% had committed violent crimes against people.

The researchers also compared matched groups of abusers and non-abusers over a 20-year period. They found the **abusers** were five times more likely to commit violent crimes than the non-abusers.

Resources

- Author's website: www.SolveMyCase.com
- Dr. Erika Karohs, website: www.Karohs.net
- Karen Weinberg, Founder of CHAI, website www.ChaiUniversal.org
- Kimon Ianetta, website: www.TrialRun.com
- Handwriting-L, website: www.Handwriting.org

- Author's favorite Serial Killer site is located at www.crimezzz.net/serialkillers

Read more about the relationship between
- Pet-Abuse.com: "Animal Cruelty and Interpersonal Violence" at www.Pet-Abuse.com as well as additional animal protection resources including an amazing database so you can search for animal abusers in your area..

If you contact any of the above please tell them you found it in this book or were referred by the author directly. *Many times they will give you a special price.*

Hotlines

CHILD ABUSE	
Judge Baker Children's Center - Child Abuse	(800) 792-5200
Child Help USA National Child Abuse hotline	(800) 422-4453
Covenant House	(800) 999-9999
RAPE AND SEXUAL ASSAULT	
Rape, Abuse, and Incest National Network	(800) 656-HOPE
Domestic Violence/Child Abuse/ Sexual Abuse	(800) 799-7233
DOMESTIC VIOLENCE	
National Domestic Violence Hotline	(800) 799-7233
National US Child Abuse Hotline	(800) 422-4453
ANIMAL ABUSE	
ASPCA	(800) 582-5979

INDEX

TO ORDER MORE COPIES OF THIS BOOK please contact us via www.SolveMyCase.com

Made in the USA
Lexington, KY
08 January 2014